ONCE AND FUTURE QUEEN

Constellina Book One

C. M. Hano

Once And Future Queen
Constellina Book One

Printed in the United States of America

Cover Design By: Jennifer Vicknair
Formatting by: Charlotte Brassington and Sue Allerton
Map Created By: V. M. Jaskerina (http://www.vmjaskiernia.com/)

First Printing, 2022
ISBN: 979-8-9853890-4-3
C.M. Hano Books
Kingsland, GA USA
www.cmhanoauthor.org

FOREWORD

This book is not suitable for any audience under the age of 18. This book contains explicit language, graphic violence, detailed sex scenes, and the mention of a past rape. Kidnapping, torture, and death are also included in this book. All sexual content is consensual between the Female Main Character and Male Main Character.

Please do not read this book if you feel that any of this content may trigger for you. I want all my readers to enjoy this adventure to their fullest.

For anyone who has ever felt that they do not deserve to be loved, know that you are worthy

CHAPTER I

GWEN

THE WHISPERING WINDS CARRY the temptation of
secrets and the light from the moon illuminates the illusions cast by our enemies. By coming here, I went against the
Regent's orders, not that I cared to abide by *that* hypercritical
bastard.

Curiosity had brought me further from the palace than
usual, but the brutal attacks had gone too far this time. The
cities are in disarray, rebellions starting in locations all over
the land, leaving the court in chaos, which is why I'm here.

Escaping.

I check the time on my watch, noticing it's well past
midnight. The window of opportunity would be here at any
second, the time of night when the illusions falter, allowing
passage between territories. Only fools would attempt what
I'm planning, but I'm no fool. I know what lies beyond the
wall: dragon shifters.

A wave of adrenaline seizes me at the thought, and I focus on the task ahead. I have been planning this for months, meticulously plotting each move I'll make up to the last second. And now, with the finish line only a few feet ahead, I'm not stopping. Especially with the scolding I will face in the morning.

I run my sweaty palms down the front of my shirt as I inhale steadily, wrestling my nerves under control. My heart slams into my chest as I watch the moonbeam spear through the center of the wall, opening the portal.

The leaves crunch under my leather boots as I pump my arms, sprinting hard, my boots digging into the ground with each step. I slam into the wall, hard, before I am propelled backwards, landing on my ass.

"Fuck!" I exclaim as my back shudders on impact, the hard ground knocking the wind from my lungs.

Getting to my feet, I cannot help but feel slightly defeated. My plan to get across the wall failed. I wasn't counting on the added magic, another illusion, I suppose. The distant sounds of cackling echoes in my ears. *Diliha.*

"That was a good one, my friend." The brunette comes sauntering over to me. Adorned in her Ombre Court colors from head to toe, with a yellow shirt tucked into brown pants and boots.

"You stick out like a sore thumb," I grumble at her. My friend smirks at me, showing her pearly white teeth, a bright contrast against her rose-colored cheeks.

"Is my black cape not dark enough?" she asks, feigning fear. "Come on, Gwen, don't tell me that getting knocked on your ass kills your sense of humor?" she asks. Short for Gwenyfer, she and my other best friend, Victoria, have called me that since childhood. "No, I just thought today would be different."

"What do you hope to achieve by getting over there?"

I shrug, looking back at the Wall of Illusion. The barrier that keeps us away from the Dracane Kingdom and deprives my people of any reprieve from the daily abuse we get from raiders, said to be from King Outher's territory.

"Honestly, I'm hoping the King will come back and get his gangs out of my Court."

"Has it gotten that bad? I mean, I've heard some things through the grapevine, but you know how nobles' gossip." Diliha must know, or else she wouldn't be asking such open-ended questions.

"Come on, Diliha, I mean, I'm sure your Council in Arian Court has discussed it more than you are leading on. Our Sagittarian Court is not much of a kingdom lately. The five cities are under attack from the criminals that live within it. I just want to do more with my life than be at Court." I brush my hand through my charcoal curls that my father says matched my mother's perfectly when I was born.

"I understand…"

"Do you? I heard about your pending engagement with the Prince of Scorpion Court." She looks down at her shuffling feet before meeting my eyes and sighing. "I haven't even met the guy. What if he's ugly?" She says with a gasp. I roll my eyes at her melodramatic response.

"I know it will be good for my kingdom, but Gwen, I'm only twenty-three. Why would I want to marry a stranger?"

"Is this something your parents wanted for you, you know, before they were…" I cannot say the word. That day haunts everyone in Constellina.

"What? Murdered? You may as well say it. It happened to

all our parents."

"That can all change."

She laughs, before speaking, "How? If I don't marry him, the treaty will act against my people. I wish, well, I guess it doesn't really matter. Wishes don't come true anymore. Not for royals."

I look at my defeated friend and realize she is right about all of it. The one relic that could grant wishes was lost long before our parents were born.

Our once great continent is now divided into five separate Courts with an enormous wall of magic separating us from the sixth, most vile Court. But that didn't stop the bad from sowing their seeds into the cities within my Court. My Father did his best to chase them out of the kingdom or imprison them for their treacherous crimes, but all efforts failed.

Until yesterday.

"Gwen, I heard about the proposition given to you."

"Don't." I put my hand up to stop her. "I don't really want to talk about it."

"Come on, Gwen, not even with your best friend? Do I need to get Tori to join us?" I smile at the mention of the third person in our little trio of rebel Princesses. Victoria, Tori for short, is a Princess of the Valerian Court—the southernmost territory of our realm.

"No, I can handle this one on my own." I tell her as my watch buzzes, alerting me of the time. "I should head back before the Lord Regent finds me missing."

"He does bed checks at this hour?" I nod and she shudders. "When your father named Warren as temporary ruler, I thought it was the dumbest mistake of his entire reign."

"Agreed. Not only is he a perverted creep with a snaggle

tooth, but he has a little turtle that follows him everywhere." She shudders again before reaching out to hug me. "Are you going to be okay getting back?"

"Yes," she replies, releasing me.

"Please text me when you get there safely."

"I will, I promise.

CHAPTER 2

GWEN

"*PRINCESS GWENYFER*, WE NEED you to be on your best behavior today. You must not forget what is at stake." Warren's voice slices through the thoughts running rampant in my head as I sit in front of my breakfast—eggs benedict and coffee with extra sugar. "Are you even listening to me?"

"Yes, but if you don't let me finish my coffee before you say any more, you will not have a tongue left to annoy me with."

"An outburst like that cannot happen," he says sternly, before sighing. I ignore him, embracing the feeling of the warm, caffeinated sugar flowing down my throat. "*He* will not tolerate this kind of behavior, and there is nothing I can do to stop him from retaliating against you." *He* is Prince Mauris of the Lirian Court, who is coming to visit today. Hence why the Lord Regent's panties are in such a twist.

I cut my eyes to Warren's. "Do you know why you have brown eyes? It's because you're full of shit."

He responds with a growl from my right side, which is no surprise. However, the boney fingers that suddenly grip my throat and the sharpened tip of a dagger pointing directly over my heart certainly are.

"You will not speak to me in such a disrespectful tone." He squeezes tighter, and I look defiantly into his eyes, a snarl of my own coming to life. "I am the ruler of this pathetic excuse for a kingdom, and the sooner I can get rid of you, the better. Don't test me, *Gwen*." I watch as his eyes wander down the neckline of my shirt, then back up to my face. "I can and will have you locked away for insubordination."

I smile at him before gripping his wrist and digging my nails into it. He winces, releasing me as I get to my feet. My eyes burn with tears as the blade cuts through me, but I ignore the pain.

"The only thing about my kingdom that is pathetic—is you!" The warm trickle of my blood coats my breast and stomach, but I will not back down. "I am the rightful ruler of this Queendom, and I will take it back, without you, or any man, at my side. Now get your filthy hands off me or I will have them removed."

He lets me go, snickering at the way my blood now coats his dagger. I grimace as he raises the blooded dagger to his mouth, flicking his tongue across it as he smirks.

"Remember this, Princess, until you are married and have an heir in your belly, I will rule over the Sagittarian Court," he says before taking his leave. Once I'm alone in the breakfast hall, I allow the tears of pain to fall. I lift my shirt, investigating what he did. Blood trails from the top of my right breast all the way down my side, stopping just above my navel.

"Fucking bastard." I hiss as I take some napkins, soaking them in the water before proceeding to clean myself up. "Not deep enough to scar but should leave a nice scab for a couple of days."

I hear a purring sound and look over to see Luma's white furred paw reaching out to me.

"I'm okay, girl." I scratch the back of cat-like ears and she rubs against the palm of my hand. "Don't worry, he will get his just deserts soon enough. Karma is a bitch, and she always bites back."

"My lady!" The doors burst open, and one guard comes running through them. He bows, although his breathing is heavy and sweat coats his features.

"What is it?"

"You have company," he says, not meeting my eye. Already? I'm still not properly dressed, and my shirt has blood on it. But then again, I don't give two shits who sees me like this. I'm a fucking warrior and will wear my blood with pride.

"Send them in." I push the plate of eggs and bread away, reaching for a green apple instead. Pulling out the dagger from my boot, I prop my feet up against the wooden tabletop as I carve slices out, popping them into my mouth.

"I just don't like him." I know that voice. Turning, I catch sight of Tori, dressed in her polar bear furs.

"Tori," I exclaim, setting my apple and dagger down before running to hug her. She hugs me back tightly.

"Told you she needed to see you." I opened my eyes, not realizing I had closed them, as Diliha walked in right behind her.

"What are you two doing here?" I ask them as we all walk

over to my table.

"We know what today is, and we wanted to be here for support. Or backup," Tori says, taking furs, now covered in my blood, off to reveal a navy-blue shirt, black pants, and ivory-colored boots. The bejeweled crown atop her head glistens under the light of the chandelier.

She doesn't seem to care that I got blood on her clothes again.

"You should have called me," I scold them both, because really, that's what modern technology is for.

"Well, we wanted to surprise you and... good heavens, is that blood? Where did that come from?" Diliha exclaims.

"Warren wanted to play with knives this morning." I smiled, hiding my fear at the memory of the dagger nicking my torso. Fear does not do anyone any favors.

"Gods, I can't wait until he is gone," Tori states. "I should kill him for you. Or hire someone."

"Tori, murder is the last resort," Diliha replies.

"I plan to have his head once I sit on my throne," I tell them, they smile in response. The three of us, lone wolves fighting for our rights in a world of men. We were all born within a month of each other. The Gods destined our friendship themselves, just as much as the deaths of our parents.

"Well, Gwen, what are you going to do about *you know who?*" Tori whispers.

"Tell him to shove it up his ass, because under the laws set forth by the first King, being unmarried shouldn't stop me from reigning over my Court. I'm of age to rule. As are you two," I tell them. I'm twenty-four, meaning I can become a Queen without a King.

"You know we don't have that privilege. Our territories

need the unions promised to us," Diliha says, a sad look on her face.

"Wouldn't the peace treaty help this kingdom, too?" Tori asks me. I have already considered the benefits it could bring to my people. But I also had to consider the harm it could do.

"The risk isn't worth it," I answer.

"That's your choice. Regardless, we are here to support you," Tori states. "How much time do we have to get you looking like a sin wrapped in pink?" I look down at my watch and notice it's noon—an extremely late start because of my midnight adventure.

"About six hours," I answer.

"Good. Let's get started."

ALEX

"Please! Please! I have a wife!"

Another poor excuse for a man. Trying to use his home life to get out of the punishment he rightfully deserves. I'm not a saint, I'm a god damned killer, and I do what is necessary for the people of this kingdom to thrive. Being the Mafia King of the Sagittarian Court cities has earned the fear and respect from those who try to defy my rules. I control laws, the money, and supplies coming in and out of this place. The humans here are pathetic and need to be properly ruled over.

Blood pools on the floor below my feet as I look at the face of yet another pathetic predator. This one was hoarding pictures of children in his house.

"We have three rules. Name them," Morgan—my sister, my right-hand woman and best friend, demands.

"Don't lie, cheat, or steal," he sputters through his swollen lips. I don't need to say or do anything but watch as she bashes the bat across his head once more.

"Try again," she growls. Morgan Pendragon is a four-foot-nothing badass, with all the bites of her inner beast and bigger balls than half the men in the entire realm. She is my general, and I, her King. If someone falls out of line, she deals with it before it gets back to me—that's how our ranking works.

On orders given to me by my Father, King Outher, I started this gang. His intentions were destructive, but ever since he showed me his true colors, I decided I would defy him in any way I could. He wants the human cities to be ruined, shifters planted throughout the Courts for when the war begins. Every pawn in his pocket is being put to use, but I don't agree with him. Not all humans are evil.

"I… I don't remember." I watch with a stoic expression as blood drips from his mouth, painting the gray concrete of his basement crimson.

"I should kill you where you lay. Gut you from neck to navel, then burn you alive for the scum you are," she snarls at him, and a small smirk forms on my face. I love watching her work. I get a sense of pride at seeing how far my apprentice has come.

"Just kill me," he pleads, and she gives me the look. The one that means it's time for me to decide this fucker's fate. Getting to my feet, I straighten the sleeves of my black suit and take a few steps forward.

"Rule number one: No fucking with innocent children," I state. My tone is deadly calm. His eyes widen with fear as my blue ones bore into him. "Rule number two: no hurting innocent women. And rule number three: you break any of my rules, and I break you."

"I'm sorry. Please, just give me another chance." I smirk—he knows what is coming next.

"Go to hell." I summon my fire, burning him where he lays until nothing but ash and soot remains. "Be sure that his wife is compensated. There is no need for her to suffer because of him any longer."

"Yes, boss." One of Morgan's loyal workers replies before getting to work cleaning up the mess. I turn on my heel, heading out of the basement, taking the stairs two at a time, and out of that cursed house.

Morgan follows not too far behind, and we make our way down the busy street until we reach one of my many establishments.

The bouncer nods at me before opening a black metal door. Inside is a small alcove leading to a tight spiral staircase that flows up to a lounge area and through the door to my office.

The walls hum, the noise pulsing from downstairs. I walk onto the plush crimson carpet, making my way to the china cabinet that holds all my personal liquor and crystal glasses. I take out the brandy and two glasses, pour the drinks and hand one to my sister before returning the brandy to the cabinet.

I sip on my drink with my back turned—allowing the burn to warm my bitter heart ever so slightly before I continue with my business for the rest of the day.

"What's next on the agenda?" Morgan asks, following me as I head to my office. All the windows are painted black, ensuring privacy from wandering eyes. You never know who you can trust these days. Morgan closes the door after us as I take a seat in front of my mahogany desk.

"We have a meeting with the Prince of the Lirian Court and the Lord Regent from the Sagittarian Court."

"We? You want me to attend them with you?" She asks in disbelief.

"Sis, I am meeting with two of the most powerful people in all of Constellina. I would like to have my general at my side."

"I'm not so sure they will welcome me to your little meeting. You know how they feel about the other sex." She sips on her whiskey, and I take a sidelong glance at her. Her pink hair is in a pixie cut so that it brushes the pointed tip of her ears and compliments the purple color of her eyes. My sister got most of her fae beauty from our mother.

"I don't care. The meeting is mutually beneficial. If they have a problem with you being there, then so be it."

"What is this one about, dear brother?" She asks, placing her empty glass on the coaster atop my desk.

"They have a proposition for me. One that will fill our banks for an exceptionally long time," I tell her, placing my hands on my desk.

"Drugs? Weapons? What do they want from you?"

"I'm not sure yet. The meeting will be held here within the hour."

"They didn't tell you anything?" I shook my head. If I have learned anything from my time amongst nobles, it's that they are corrupt, conniving bastards that would rather see their cities defiled by the scum of the world than deal with it head on. The human men seem to enjoy taking advantage of women. They'll be foolish to try that with her.

"That is dangerous. What if they mean to set a trap? Or plot your murder to right the wrong that was done to the realm by Father?"

"That's why you're coming with me. We are fae, they are humans. I would say we have the upper hand, wouldn't you?" I ask her. She nods. "I will hear what they offer, but it does not mean I will agree to it. We could definitely use the money."

"What do you mean? Last I checked, we had plenty."

"We *had* until our cousins went to war with one another." We have six cousins, five males and one female.

Each leader runs their cities with their own rules. We all avoid disrupting each other, however, recent events have brought to light a development between the gangs within the Arian Court.

"Which ones? And why?" She asks.

"Lawrence and Junior have decided they want one leader in charge of all of Arian Court. They want to have one ruler, just as I am here. Not that I give a shit what happens to them, but Father clarified we must take over control of all the Courts by any means necessary. If they are waging war against each other, who is running their cities?"

"Has our Father received this news yet?" She asks.

"I believe he is aware," I answer as I take out my phone to run through that last message he sent me.

Sperm Donor:
Is this going to be a problem? Because if I must cross over before it is time, then so help me, I will make you pay.

"Alright, what's the plan?" I look up at her and smirk.

"I'm glad you are so willing to help, because as soon as this meeting is over, I would like to send you to Arian Court to knock some sense into your dear cousins before I have to take matters into my own hands."

"You want me to leave your side?"

"Do you think I am incapable of taking care of myself?"

"No, but…" she pauses, "I have been here with you since I was fourteen, learning the ins and outs of being a part of your gang. I haven't seen our cousins in over a decade. Why do you expect them to listen to me?"

I hate it when she doubts herself.

"Morgan, I named you my general for a reason. You are smart, cunning, and strong. Your loyalty to me is unwavering, and you are capable of things you don't even know. That's why I'm trusting this to you." I pause before getting to my feet and turn to face the large map pinned to the back of the wall. "This realm has been in chaos since we were children. Our Father has been trying to unite all the Courts for three decades. But the humans will not listen to reason, their ignorance blinding them."

"What Father wants is a dictatorship, not peace or prosperity."

"I know. So, what do we do about it?" I smirk. Her eyes go wide as she guesses what I'm thinking.

"You're not suggesting a mutiny, are you?"

"No, the Wall of Illusions protects this side of the world from Father's armies. He means to destroy it, and use me to do so. I mean to defy him."

"But why?"

"Because, dear sister, what do you think will happen to us, to our little kingdom, if he is successful? Do you think he will let me remain the Mafia King? What of our cousins?" I step backwards, turning towards my desk to open the top drawer and pull out the paper I have been holding on to for the last month. "Come and see."

I unravel the paper just as her shoulder brushes against mine. "Is that what I think it is?"

"The Golden Sun. Indeed, we are going to steal it. With its power, I can rid the world of Outher Pendragon and become the Dracane King. Under my reign, there will be peace, because I will sit down with each monarch and offer them something they cannot refuse."

"Which is?"

"Peace for profit."

"You mean to bribe them? We do not have enough money to do that."

"Not yet, but once I complete whatever task our visitors will ask of me, I'm sure we will." I smirk at her. "Are you still with me, darling sister?" She ponders it for a moment, and her hesitation has me worried.

"It's a bat shit crazy plan, but I'm with you to the end." We high five like the friends we are. "I will go once your meeting is complete."

"Thank you."

CHAPTER 3

ALEX

"GENTLEMEN, MAY I OFFER you a brandy?" Morgan asks the Lirian Court Prince and the Lord Regent.

"No, thank you. I wish to keep my wits about me while in the presence of the most powerful man in all the kingdom." The Lord Regent's false flattery is pitiful, and I give him the 'I'm not falling for your bullshit' look.

"What do you want?" I ask them both as they sit in front of me.

"Straight and to the point, I like it," The Lord Regent states, smirking at the quiet royal. "As I am sure you are aware, the Princess will be of age soon," he pauses, gauging my reaction, and when I do not give him one, he clears his throat and continues. "Which means it will be time for her coronation and for her to become Queen."

The room remains quiet as I give him a stoic expression.

Is he really going to ask me what I think he is? "I need to ensure that she never becomes the Queen."

Yes, a total dick move. I have no qualms with the Princess.

"And why should I care?" The question catches him off guard, judging from the look of astonishment on his face.

"Well, because she is a woman. Women are not meant to rule. They are meant—"

"And what's that?" Morgan cuts in. I glance over at her and note the killer look in her eyes.

"Alexxander, a man of your stature can surely appreciate—" I cut off his air with the death grip I have around his scrawny neck, baring my teeth at him in a low growl.

"Ignore my sister again, and I will slit your throat. Understand?" He nods, then stumbles as I push him away, clutching at his throat. My eyes look towards the Prince, who seems unbothered by our brief confrontation, so I decide to ignore the misogynistic bastard and direct my next question to the royal prick warming one of my chairs.

"Tell me, Prince Mauris, what business brought you here today? If it is solely because a woman is going to become a Queen, then save your breath. I will not hear it." He looks at me with brown eyes.

"My business is my own. I have no issue with the Queen except that she dies before her next birthday," he states passionately, making me wonder what she did to piss him off.

"What was her crime?"

"Not hers, but her father's."

"And why are you punishing the daughter for the sins of her father?"

He takes a deep breath before answering. "Her father is responsible for the death of my parents. I seek justice, not just vengeance."

"That sounds like the same thing to me. Has she been put on trial?"

"I don't need one. I have evidence. A witness from that day."

"And I assume that once this witness gives me all the details, you expect me to just carry out an assassination? Do you think I'm that foolish?"

"I do not. That is why I brought this memory potion, so you may use it on them."

I rub my chin, curious about this rare magical element. "How did you gain it? I was told it is only sold by fae witches in the Dracane Kingdom." He smirks at me.

"Do not think that you are the only powerful person with connections to the other side. Your father wants her gone just as much as I do." I shoot a look towards Morgan, who gives me a don't trust them, look.

"Anyone who deals with my father is not to be trusted."

"But you deal with him."

"Precisely. But, since you are so adamant about this, I will hear your witness and see their memories before I decide."

"Good, because they are here and ready." Before I can respond, the doors to my office open and an older woman enters. "Alexxander, I would like to introduce you to Patrice. She was a servant during King Robert's reign." She bows before me, before taking Mauris's seat.

"I am ready," she croaks. I watch her as she drinks the rare relic, her eyes glowing white as her memories are projected above her head. The events of that day play out in front of me. Each monarch drinking from a chalice of wine before dropping dead to the floor. When it's over, I look at our three guests, then back to my sister, who just shrugs. She obviously doesn't care what I decide.

"Fine. When does this need to be completed, and how much are you willing to pay?"

"I will pay you six billion if you can do it tonight," Mauris replies.

"Why so soon?"

"Because she turns twenty-four in two weeks, and I am to meet her this evening at six," he pauses for a moment before continuing. "We are discussing a peace treaty that involves uniting our Courts in holy matrimony."

"I see. So, not only do you want her dead because of what her father did, but because you do not want to marry her. Am I correct?"

"Yes." Killing a royal is no small task. Especially a Princess. They are typically well guarded. Not that I can't sneak in and out of places unnoticed, however, it means this is a job I will do on my own.

"Very well. Just one more question, has she ever met you before? Does she know what you look like?"

"No," he answers, confused.

"Good." Before they even know what is happening, Morgan has all three of them unconscious and on the floor. "Put them in the dungeons. Wipe their memories. I don't want any loose ends when all this is said and done."

"Are you really going to go kill this woman?" She asks me.

"No, but I am going to have a pleasant chat with her. She has never met Mauris, nor has she met me. I will glamor my looks to appear as a human. She will be none the wiser." I feel her hand on my shoulder and I turn towards her. Concern laces her features.

"Please be careful, Alex. I don't know what I would do without you." I clasp her other shoulder.

"You and I will both be fine. After dealing with these three, please deal with our cousins." I press a kiss to her forehead before looking at my watch.

Be ready Princess, for I am a beast that a beauty will never tame.

GWEN

Tonight, I am going to be on my best behavior.

Or so the Lord Regent has requested. Much to his dismay, that is the exact opposite of what I plan to be—I even dressed the part. I'm wrapped in a tight pink dress that fits my curves perfectly, the slits on either side of my skirt exposing my tanned legs all the way to my upper thigh. The draping neckline exposes the sides of my breasts—not very lady-like, but really, why should I care?

I have never conformed to the standards of a royal. It's my right as a human, to choose what and how I dress—even if it means exposing a little skin. My choice of footwear is ankle black leather boots, allowing me to store my smallest dagger inside, and my hair is curled into waves that flow down my back, pinned at the back of my head with a small dagger clip. My half-updo is compliments of Tori, but I chose the finishing piece—rose-gold glasses instead of my regular contacts.

"Damn, Gwen, have you seen yourself lately?" Diliha comments, ogling my reflection.

"I look good, don't I?"

"Good? Girl, everyone will drool over you tonight. Women and men." Tori winks at me. "But I have one question," she pauses, "Why did you decide to wear your glasses? You usually avoid them."

"I have recently overcome that insecurity because nerds are hot, and if my near-sightedness is a flaw, so be it. I'm tired of society trying to tell women about how we are supposed to look. We are Princesses, we have a power that other women do not. I would like to show our world that having glasses and curves is perfectly acceptable." I sigh. "Besides, the contacts bother my eyes after a few hours."

"Well, I think both Tori and I can get on board with that. Let us show these people we don't give a fuck about societal standards." Diliha smiles as she pulls out two more dresses from her bag that match mine—an auburn one, the color of her Court, and a deep satin blue color for Tori.

"You two are my greatest treasures, I hope you know that?" I tell them. "Now get ready. We don't want to be late. I'm meeting my future husband tonight."

As we stand right outside the throne hall doors, I link arms with my girls, Tori on my right, Diliha on my left. I feel empowered in this moment—what we are about to do will set in motion a chorus of events.

"Princess." A soft voice comes from behind us somewhere and we all turn to search for its source. Scampering down the hall in a panic is Bianca, my lady's maid. When she catches up to us, her breath is heavy, and she has something in her hands.

"Bianca, is everything okay?" I ask, unlocking my arms from the girls and turning. I take a step towards her and rub her back, hoping to ease whatever has her panicked.

"Thank you, Your Highness, but I only rushed because I thought I might not catch you in time."

"In time for what?" She lifts her head, her breathing seeming to steady.

"The Lord Regent, he changed the night's events from a dinner party to a masquerade." I furrow my brows. "Forgive me, but I have these for you three." She reaches out her hands, holding three beautiful masks.

"Bianca, did you make these?" I ask, taking one from her and running my fingers over the exquisite craftsmanship. The one I'm holding is white with small, bejeweled diamonds embedded along the seam.

"I did. The gems are fake, but I got word a few hours ago and went straight to work," she admits. I take the white one, while Tori picks up a black one, leaving Diliha one in a reddish purple.

"A few hours ago? Why didn't you come tell me?"

"Forgive me, I assumed that the Lord Regent had already informed you." Bianca bows her head in shame.

"No harm done. Thank you, Bianca." She lifts her head and smiles. "We should get going."

"How are you going to wear that over your glasses?" Tori asks.

"I'm not. I will not hide my face to appease that creep of a man. But if you two wish to partake in this masquerade, I will not pass any ill judgment." Tori smiles and Diliha squeals excitedly.

We turn back towards the double oak doors, and I gesture for the guards to open them. With my mask clutched in my right hand at my side, I take a step forward. My best friends' movements coordinated with mine as we parted the crowd of masked figures. I spare no one a glance as we march straight towards the front of the room where I usually stand at events such as these.

"Your Highnesses," Sir Palitine bows his head in greeting. Even behind his golden mask, I know who he is by the scar running across his right eye. Not that he has that eye anymore. It was taken out by an attack from one of those barbaric dragon shifters.

"Where is Warren?" I ask him.

"He is currently busy. Something to do with important matters of state."

"This was his idea, and he doesn't even have the decency to show his face. Typical," I sigh, before turning to face the crowd. From the raised platform, I can see that I'm, in fact, the only one here not adorning a mask. I scan the room for any sign of my potential husband, but truth be told, I have no clue what he looks like.

Tonight, was about us announcing our engagement after agreeing to a treaty that would allow his armies to rid my cities of the gangs that litter its streets with crime and death. Once my Queendom was at peace again, our countries would merge into one. But I don't just want peace and prosperity for my people.

This marriage would be one of convenience, nothing more, but I have a proposition for my potential husband that I want to run by him. One that I hope would interest him as much as it does me. I cannot exactly do that now since all the men have dressed in tuxedos of varying colors of their Courts and, of course, the women did the same.

Except us three.

"Your Highness." I look over and see a man dressed in a black suit with an emerald green vest underneath the suit jacket and a matching mask. The colors compliment his black hair and bronzed skin tone. "May I have this dance?"

Diliha looks over at me for permission and I nod. It is not my wish tonight for my friends to miss mingling with eligible bachelors. Although we are all potentially engaged to others, it doesn't mean we can't have a little fun.

Not a second later, Tori is being escorted to the dance floor by a masked man from the Arian Court. While I watch my friends dance amongst the patrons, I admire the decorative crystal chandeliers hanging from the domed ceiling. The orchestra plays an upbeat waltz while servants hand out filled flute glasses to the other guests that are socializing on the outskirts of the dance floor.

"Penny for your thoughts." A deep voice comes from my right side, catching me off-guard. When I turn, my breath catches at the man standing before me. Adorned in an all-black suit, with deep, amber-colored eyes, and sun-kissed skin, is the most stunning man I have ever seen. The mask he wears leaves nothing to the imagination, to include the stubble that lines the squareness of his jaw and the plump nature of his lips.

Lips that have my thoughts running rampant at the thought of how they would feel pressed against my skin. A warmth fills my chest. My eyes trail down his body from the black color of his hair, down to the shine radiating from his dress shoes.

"Your Highness?" He tilts his head sideways as if he is assessing me with just as much admiration as I just did to him.

"What?" I croak as my mouth feels bone dry. I swallow hard before pulling myself together. "I need a drink."

I make a beeline for the first servant I see, scooping up a filled glass flute and gulping down the chardonnay that does nothing to help with my parched mouth. *What is the matter with you? You act like you have never seen a man before.* I roll my shoulders, regaining my composure.

"Are you well?" I turn and see that he has followed me, a smirk playing at the corner of his mouth.

"Yes. And now I must be on my way," I state before turning to head to the buffet at the far-right side of the room.

"I thought I would ask you for a dance." He says, forcing me to stop mid-step.

"You thought wrong."

"Are you always like this?"

"Like what?" I cross my arms, the heat I felt for him dissipating quickly.

"Rude to your people." He tilts his head sideways again.

"No, I am not. Forgive me." I was quite rude; I will give him that, but only because I was caught off-guard for the first time since I could remember.

"Dance with me, and we will forget about it." He smirks, revealing a dimple in his right cheek. I take his out-stretched hand and we glide over to the dance floor.

His hand snakes around my waist, his fingers close around my hand, holding me close to his chest as the music slows. He stands two-feet taller than me, leaving my line of sight on his overly broad chest. I don't need to see him naked to know it's most likely well defined with muscle. *Why am I thinking about him naked?*

"Look at me," he whispers, and I tilt my chin up to meet his eyes. "A woman as beautiful as you should never shy away."

I feel the heat rising in my cheeks, but I brush it off with a snarky remark. "If you think calling me beautiful will get you anywhere with me, you're mistaken."

He leans forward to whisper in my ear, his scent is a mix of ash and pine, "Believe me, Princess, if I was trying to get anywhere with you, you'd know it."

When I go to speak, I'm suddenly spun out of his arms, and then right back against his chest. His breath is hot against my neck, alighting my skin just as his hard grip on my hip tightens. He hums in my ear before letting me go so we can go back to our normal stance.

"You know I could have you thrown in the dungeons for pulling that move?" I ask as we continue to move to the rhythm.

"Don't threaten me with a fun time, Princess." His remark surprises me and I realize that is the fourth time he has stunned me in just one song. A song that seems to drag on and on.

"Who are you?" I ask, searching his eyes for an answer.

"I'm no one."

I let out a sarcastic laugh, "I highly doubt that. the Lord Regent doesn't invite *nobodies* to events such as these."

"And are you privy to all the things your Lord Regent does?" I stop my movements and relinquish my grip on him, but he doesn't do the same to me.

"How dare you ask me a question like that?"

"So, you are not."

"Release your grip on me." I bare my teeth at him.

"No," he bites back.

"Very well." If he thinks I'm going to call for the guards, he's mistaken. It may not be very ladylike of me to do this in front of everyone, but he asked for it. Rearing back my fist, I punch him square in the jaw before kneeing him in the gut. He falls to the floor, clutching his side. When he looks at me again, a full-on smile spreads across his face.

"Gwen, are you okay?" I turn to see Tori at my side.

"Nothing I couldn't handle on my own." I smirk at him as he rises to his feet. "You are done here. Leave my Court."

"But I'm not done talking to you yet." I scoff at the audacity of this man thinking he can still converse with me after that.

"You're asking for trouble."

"No, I'm asking for only one conversation, that's all." His look has gone from humorous to intense in a blink of an eye.

"Get. Out," I growl, and he closes the distance between us. Towering over me with a glare that should intimidate me, but it doesn't.

"No." I see the defiance in his eyes and know he will not go willingly.

"Shall I call for the guards?" Tori asks, but I don't break my eye contact with Mr. Man.

"No, I will escort him out personally," I tell her before gesturing towards the door. "If you wish to speak, speak quickly."

"The speed of my tongue is good for only one thing, Princess." I ignore him by stepping past him and biting the inside of my cheek to prevent the blush threatening to rise at the obvious innuendo of his statement. What would it feel like to have that mouth pressed against my lips?

I hear his footfall behind me as the crowd parts. I ignore the hushed whispers and estrange looks as I make my way to the doors.

"I don't hear you speaking. Your time is dwindling." I don't spare a glance over my shoulder because I couldn't give two shits if he is going to talk. Once the doors open, I don't stop until I hear them shut. I go to turn around, only to have a hand covering my mouth and a thick arm wrap around my waist, pressing me against a hard chest.

"Now that I have your undivided attention, there are some grievances we need to discuss." Yeah, this shit will not happen to me. What are my guards doing? Out of the corner of my eye, they are nowhere to be found. Without further thinking, I stomp down on his foot before thrusting my elbow into his gut. Only I'm stopped when pain shoots up my arm.

"What the fuck?" It comes out muffled against his hand and then I bite down hard until I can taste the copper tang of blood, but he doesn't let up.

"Oh, Princess, you are testing my self-restraint today. But if you want to play rough, we can do that later," he growls. I don't release my teeth from his skin, and he doesn't seem to care. "Now we are taking a little trip. I would like for you to be cooperative, but if you keep acting like a brat, I will have to knock you out."

"Fuck you," I mutter against his palm as my teeth break free.

"I might take you up on that, but right now, I just need to talk."

"I'm going to slit your throat," I threaten, he hums as if he's enjoying this, and then I feel it. Pressing against my ass is his hardened cock. "You're a crazy bastard."

"I've been called worse." We move down the corridor. His grip on me is iron steel. If only I could get to my daggers. A thought crosses my mind and I allow my body to become dead weight, which catches him by surprise. We take a tumble to the floor, and I try to get away from him. As we roll, I reach my right boot, praising the Gods when the cool hilt touches my palm. Gripping it, I pull it out and find myself straddled on top of him.

The mask falls from his face, and I get to see the pure beauty of him. I press my blade across his throat but feel him grip my hips as he flips us. My knife makes a cut, but it does not seem to faze him one bit. I watch as red droplets ooze from his neck.

"This is not how I pictured your first time pinned beneath me, but I have no complaints."

"You're a pig."

"And you, princess, have cut me."

"Get off of me."

"I don't think you want me to."

"You're delusional."

"If you wanted me gone so badly, you would've called for your guards." I freeze for a moment, thinking he was right, but that was a mistake as he wrenches my dagger from my hand, pins my arms above my head with one hand, and examines the blade.

"This is an exquisite little thing. Where did you get it?"

"Get off me." He looks at me and then drags the tip of the blade across my cheek, down my throat, and then down the valley of my breasts. My nipples harden and wetness pools between my legs.

"On one condition."

"You are in no position to ask anything of me."

"Hmm, I believe I am. Seeing as you are underneath me and I have your little dagger." He moves it across the fabric covering my nipples and smirks.

"Are you turned on?" He grins, a dimple appearing in his cheek.

"In your dreams."

"Perhaps. While this banter is fun, we need to get on with this." Fear courses through me momentarily until he pulls me to my feet, holding the dagger to my throat as my back is pressed to the wall.

"If you are going to kill me, do it before I get the chance to kill you." I growl.

"You already had your chance." He gestures to the minor cut on his throat. "I will not kill you, princess, but I need to ask you some questions."

"And if I refuse to answer them?"

"You won't, because you will want the reward for being a *good girl*." I cringe at the thought of this man, who I still do not know, baiting me into submission.

"You chose the wrong princess if you think I will be a good girl. I am, in fact, a bad girl and I am done with you. Gua-" The metal hits me hard before I get the words out and as my vision fades, I pray to the gods that someone heard me before I was taken from this world. I pray to the gods that someone heard me.

CHAPTER 4

ALEX

I WAS RUNNING BEHIND SCHEDULE when I left for the masquerade being held at the palace.

The invitation clutched in my hand had the seal of the Lord Regent, which I swiped off his unconscious body before leaving for the tailors. I glamoured my features to hide my horns and pointed ears. When the humans look at me, they will see a man with bright blue eyes and golden hair.

When I arrived at the palace, the ball had already begun. Pushing my way through the crowd, I search for my target and notice her instantly. Long curls of black flowing down to the waistband of her pink satin dress. She has chosen not to hide her beautiful features from this room, which I am entirely grateful for.

Behind her rose gold glasses are two bright blue eyes that remind me of precious jewels. My gaze travels along the curves of her body, stopping at her chosen footwear. Boots. Comfortable and clever.

I make my way over to her but stop when another man snatches her up. The hairs on the back of my neck rise as I catch the slight tremor in his appearance. It appears I am not the only dragon shifter attending tonight.

I watch from a distance as they glide across the floor, noting the way her body reacts to him. She is not above charm magic. My fingers curl into fists at the sight of his body connected to hers.

It would be foolish of me to step in, but I am half a second from ripping her away from him. "Would you like to dance?"

My gaze cuts to the right to see a masked woman standing next to me. "No."

When I look back to where my princess was dancing, I hit myself on the head for allowing the distraction, noticing they were gone. "Where the fuck did you go?"

"Excuse me?"

"Not you." I growl before making my way through the crowd. Looking up, I notice the entry doors open and shut, but as I push forward, the crowd resists me. My fire is begging to be released the more my temper rises. Finally, I decide, fuck it, and let my voice boom through the hall. "Move!"

The chatter dies down quickly and the crowd parts. As I reach the doors, the party behind me resumes, drowning out my groan as I crack open the door and peer through. *Where the fuck are the guards?*

Stepping out, I look left and right, using my dragon sight to zoom ahead of me until my nose catches the scent of blood and my ears catch her trying to yell out. Following the scent, I make my way around the corner and then see them. Draped across his arms, unconscious, is my princess.

"Put her down." I state calmly, in a tone that would frighten most men, but this is not just any man. He turns to look at me and smirks while placing the tip of the dagger against her cheek.

"No, I don't think I will."

"If you want to leave here with your entrails intact, I suggest you listen to me."

"What's a human like you going to do to me?" Interesting, he might be a shifter, but he's a weak one if he can't detect my glamor.

"Disobey me and find out." I bait him, but he will not be leaving here alive. Not since I can see he has already hurt her. There is blood dripping from her head onto the marbled tile. "On second thought," in a flash, I have my talons deep inside his throat. His eyes are wide with shock and fear. "You can die for hurting what is mine."

I jerk my hand back while taking his throat with it. Blood splatters onto me, but I do not care as I quickly take her from his arms while he falls to the ground. His glamor fails as he dies. While looking at her face, I notice her glasses have fallen nearby.

Setting her gently on the floor, I pocket her glasses before scooping her back into my arms and making my way onto a balcony, "Don't worry, princess. You're safe with me." I allow my glamor to fall as I summon my wings. They burst from my back, and I take flight into the dark of night. Traveling by air is my preferred method, and once we are within my territory, no one will question me.

As my golden wings flap faster, I try not to focus on the slowing rhythm of her heartbeat. I have never been one to worry about such things as this, but something about her dying does not agree with me. I understand I was sent to kill her, but I do not commit cold-blooded murder. Just a conversation and that will be all I need to make my decision.

I land on the roof of my casino, which has my apartment on the top level, and make my way through the metal door that connects to the stairs that lead to my apartment door. Once inside, I ensure it is closed before laying her on the sofa. Locking the door, I move back over to her and press healing magic onto her wound.

"Don't worry princess, I've got you." I say, as a small hand fiercely grips my wrist, digging nails sharply into my skin like tiny talons.

"Get. Your hands, off me." The furious look in her blue eyes caught me by surprise. I remove my hand; having now healed her wound. She does not let me go as she has somehow pulled a dagger on me. It looks like the same one that shifter had against her, but how is that possible? "Back away."

I raise my hands in surrender. "Easy princess, I was just helping you."

"I highly doubt that. Move." She sits up as, keeping a tight grip on the hilt of her blade. Her eyes never leave me as she assesses her threat. I get to my feet and allow my glamor to fall. She gasps and chargers forward. I move at the last second before the tip can pierce my chest.

"What are you doing?" I growl as I block each strike.

"Killing a shifter." She snarls right back.

"If this is how you repay everyone that saves your life, I don't think you have very many friends." I block her next strike, grabbing her wrists and pinning it to the back wall. I expect her next move, which will be her striking a very delicate place. "Stop."

"Never." She tries to overpower me, but my strength doesn't fail.

"Why are you so angry?" I ask while she continues to struggle against my hold. The death grip she has on her dagger never falters, although I have her pinned in place against the wall. Our breath mingles between us as she still fights against me.

"Shifters are nothing but cold-blooded killers. You all deserve to die for the crimes you commit."

"And what crimes are those? Ridding your cities of all the filthy humans that live here." Her eyes go wide as she pauses for a moment. "You didn't know that the real criminals are the humans."

"Back off." She growls.

"Only if you promise to behave." I wink, but she nods. I slowly release my hold and she does not move from the spot against the wall.

"What am I doing here?" She asks. That anger not leaving a single word.

"I saved your life. Figured it was best to bring you to the safest spot in the kingdom." I tell her while leaning against the wall. My wings retracted the moment we landed. So as far as she can tell, I have horns and pointed ears.

"What do you mean?" then she reaches up to touch the healed spot on her head. "Shit, there was a guy. He attacked me. Where is he?"

"Dead." I tell her, expecting fear, even a slight quiver, but I do not get that reaction from her.

"Good. Now, how the hell do I get out of here and back to the palace?"

"You don't."

"Excuse me?" That fierceness is back as she approaches me, dagger at the ready.

"You smell lovely, princess, but if you are getting this close to me, you better be ready for what comes next." Her scent is alluring, damning, making all my self-control falter.

"Listen, shifter boy, all I want to do is get back home. I don't care about anything else."

"Even a threat to your life?" I challenge, swallowing the last of the space between us in two strides. She appears to be in disbelief at my statement and her gaze falters, but I dislike it. Gripping her chin, I raise her head up so I can look deep into her eyes. "Never do that again."

"What?" It comes out just above a whisper.

"Feel ashamed or afraid."

"Why are you being nice to me? Why did you save my life?" Her questions baffle me and raise my own. I could have easily let her die, then killed the bastard. Deepening my pockets with the reward, but something profound inside me told me not to.

"Because I have decided I like you and I want you to be mine." She gasps and I shock myself with that last admission.

Then her eyes narrow as she steps away from me. "Never. I will never be with a shifter."

"Fair enough." I shrug, "You hate me because of what King Outher has done, and I do not entirely despise you. But I will tell you this, princess," I step closer, reaching out and tucking a curl behind her ear. "Your life is in danger at that palace. The safest place in this entire realm is right here."

"How do I know you aren't lying to me?" She asks.

"You don't, but you seem like a wise human. What do your instincts tell you?" I wait for her to respond as my fingers caress her soft cheek, down the side of her neck, before I retract my hand.

"You healed my head." She states more than asks. "That tells me that if you wanted me dead, I'd be dead, but it doesn't mean I trust you."

"That's a start. I will take what I can get. In the meantime, I will get you some clothes and show you to the guest room. Are you hungry?" I turn to start moving but stop when I notice she is not. Looking over my shoulder, I see the hesitation in her eyes.

"I can't stay here." She crosses her arms, ensuring the tip of her dagger stays visible.

"Where else can you go?" I ask before turning back to face her.

"Tori's or Diliha's, they are probably worried sick about me, anyway." I dislike the thought of her leaving my sight, but if I try to hold her prisoner, this will never work.

"Agree to stay here for the night and I will help you get to their place tomorrow." It is a simple gesture, but I know it will mean a lot to her.

"Really?" She asks, raising a brow.

"If you think I kidnapped you, you are wrong." It's true that my initial plan was to kidnap her, but seeing her in the arms of another man, bleeding, it just did something to me. Awoken my inner dragon. Us dragons are highly possessive over the things we want and what I want is a feisty princess with charcoal colored hair and a killer right hook.

"Agreed." She says at last; I watch as she sheaths her dagger into her boot, my gaze following her body as I cannot help but catch how her dress reveals the plumpness of her breasts. My mouth waters at the sight and my cock stirs in my pants. I adjust my stance as she stands up. "I would like to shower first."

"Follow me." I turn quickly, trying to hide my growing erection at the thought of her naked body in my house but I do not think that getting her in my bed on the first night is a smart move because once I get a taste of her, I know I will never let her go again.

As we make our way down the short hallway, I show her the guest room, which is right across the hall from mine. "Each room has its own bathroom. I will get you some clothes and be right out."

"Thank you." She states and I turn, heading into my room. I go to my drawer to pull out a pair of boxers and a shirt. Walking back out, I see her lost in thought. I allow myself one more gaze before clearing my throat.

"There is soap and other things in the bathroom if you need it." I tell her.

"Do you bring women back here often?" She asks, almost sounding jealous. I smirk at her as I lean against the doorframe.

"If I say yes, would you be jealous?" She rolls her eyes before I see the hint of a smile begging to reveal itself.

"Not likely. I don't give two shits about who you have had in your apartment."

"Then why did you ask?" She looks at me before biting her bottom lip, making my inner dragon want to claim her for his own.

She shrugs "Curiosity."

"Here." I push the pile of clothes to her, and she takes them, our fingers brushing, eliciting a shiver from her. I am not the only one who is responsive. *I will have you as mine before you know it, princess.*

"Thank you." She bites her bottom lip again, and I cannot help but grip her chin and run my thumb across it.

"If you keep doing that, I will have no choice but to have you in my bed, pinned beneath me while I mark your body with my mouth." She shudders again, and I smell her arousal. "Why are you teasing me, princess?"

"I'm not." Her tongue darts out to lick the tip of my thumb and I cannot help the groan that leaves my throat. "What's your name?"

I look at her eyes as her question surprises me. "If I tell you my name, will you reward me with a kiss?" I want to kiss her, to know what she tastes like.

"No." She answers, and I smile.

"So resistant." I drop my hand and take a step back. "If you need anything, I'm right across the hall." I turn my back and close the door, needing to take a cold shower before I do something stupid.

GWEN

As I close the door to the guest room, I turn my back and smile to myself as I flick the light on.

"Oh, shifter boy, you have met your match." I mutter to myself triumphantly. Making my way over to the bathroom, I admire the black sheets that line the queen-sized mattress. The plush carpet beneath my boots ends when I step onto the white tile floor of the bathroom. Placing the shirt and boxers on top of the counter, I turn and look at myself in the mirror.

Dried blood coats my disheveled hair and I notice my glasses are missing. The fucker that attacked me must have crushed them. I run my hand over the spot and expect a scar or pain, but there is nothing.

"Shifter magic." I bend down to remove my socks and boots before reaching behind my back to pull the zipper of my dress down, but I can't reach it and hiss, "Fuck."

A wicked thought crosses my mind. I have never played the role of seductress and it may be stupid to do this with a shifter, but it is the perfect way to get him in irons and put on trial for being the cold-blooded killer he is.

I exit the bathroom, open the bedroom door, and pause when I see said shifter boy about ready to knock. "Is something wrong?"

"Nope."

I cross my arms and cock an eyebrow. "Then why are you standing out there ready to knock?" My gaze falls to his raised arm that bends when he grips the back of his neck. "And why aren't you wearing a shirt?" I do not shy away as my eyes move across his chiseled torso, down the defined six-pack, following the small trail of black hair travelling from his navel to below his waistband.

"Are you ogling me, princess?" I snap my eyes back up to him, but there is no use in denying it.

"Maybe." I bite my bottom lip, knowing what it does to him. "I can't reach my zipper." I turn around, pulling my hair over my shoulder as I reveal the zipper to him. As he moves closer, I feel the heat of his body.

His fingers brush against the exposed skin along my back, causing goosebumps to trail after him. I feel my dress tug slightly as he moves the zipper down slowly. I was expecting him to step back, but his hand moved to the knot at the back of my neck. I cross my arms over my chest to hold the fabric of my dress up. "Alex," he whispers in my ear, the closeness of him making my attempt at seduction all too real.

"What?"

"My name, princess." I feel the brush of his lips against my ear, and I cannot help but crane my neck to give him access. When I expect him to make a move, he steps back. I glance over my shoulder to see him retreating into his room. I already miss his warmth.

The bathroom door clicks shut behind me as I cross the room to turn the shower on. The satin of my dress pools at my feet as I step out of it and into the warm stream of water. The memory of his touch on my skin has dark thoughts running through my mind. Reverse seduction.

Fucking hell.

I cannot be attracted to him. But as I lie to myself, I know deep down that when he touched me; He set my body aflame. Awakening something inside of me.

I finish showering quickly, not wanting to be in a vulnerable position any longer than necessary. The soft towel caresses my skin as I rummage through the drawers, delighted to find unused toiletries to brush my teeth with. After braiding my hair, I loose a sigh as I pull on the shirt and boxers he gave me, trying to ignore the delicious scent of smoke and soap enveloping me. "They're clean." I jump at the sound of his voice, and he chuckles.

"What are you doing here?" I ask. He walks towards me; I notice his hair is wet, and he still is not wearing a shirt. He places his hands on either side of me on the countertop, closing me in. I should not allow this.

"You are tempting fate, princess."

"Me? You're the one who brought me here."

His eyes assess me from head to toe. "I enjoy seeing you in my clothes."

"Alex, why did you come here? If you came here because you think something is going to happen, you are wrong." His face becomes stern as he looks at me.

"I came to say goodnight." He mutters, but his eyes fall to my lips, and I assume he means to kiss me. Do I want him to?

"Goodnight." I whisper as I lean forward, a breath of air between us. He hums before stepping back and heading out of the room, leaving me breathless. I hear the door close and then a lock turn. Making my way to the door, I try the nob and find it locked. "Bastard, I thought you said you weren't kidnapping me."

"I'm not, just ensuring you stay safe."

"Fuck you."

"Only if you ask nicely." He mocks me through the door, and I cannot help but bawl my hands into fists. "You're going to have to try harder than that if you intend to seduce me."

So that is how he wants to play. Fine. Game on.

CHAPTER 5

GWEN

IWAKE UP ON a pair of fluffy dark clouds and feel serene. As I open my eyes, I pause as the unfamiliar ceiling comes into focus. The cathedral style I am used to seeing is no longer present. Throwing the sheets off, I pad across the room to try the doorknob. A smile curves my lips as I quickly peek my head out and scan the quiet hall, which is dragon shifter free.

The scent of coffee has my mouth watering. Quietly closing the door, I make my way down the hall to find the kitchen off to the right.

My eyes catch on the flexing back muscles of the shifter boy as he makes breakfast. I bite my lip as I admire his pert ass. "Good morning, princess. See anything you like?"

"Yes." I say as I stride over to the counter beside him and grab the pot of coffee. "A cup?"

He smirks at me before reaching for a cabinet above my head and pulls down a porcelain white cup. As he holds it, I keep my eyes locked on his as I pour the hot caffeinated goodness into it. I am so lost in his eyes, that I don't realize the coffee is spilling over until I see him wince.

"Shit, sorry." I put the pot back on the burner before grabbing a rag and cleaning his torso. Patting his soaked pants.

"Princess," he states through gritted teeth.

"I'm sorry."

"It's not that." He grunts, and then I feel it under my hand. My eyes drift down at the bulge in his pants from where my hand was. I jerk my hand away, my cheeks heating with embarrassment. "I knew you wanted me, but you don't need to burn me with coffee to get me. Just ask nicely."

My apologetic nature turns straight into rage. "Seriously? I don't want you."

"You sure about that, princess?" I follow his gaze and notice my nipples are peeked through the shirt. I cover them with my arms.

"So? I'm cold." Which was a complete lie. I have been anything except cold since laying eyes on him.

"Did you know I can smell when you're aroused?" He presses towards me, pinning me to the counter.

"Alex," he silences me with a finger to my lips.

"Don't lie to me because I smell it already." I feel the wetness pooling between my legs. "And you know what is so infuriating about your scent?" I shake my head, to tongue tied to speak. "It's intoxicating. The need to know if you taste as good as you smell is all I'm thinking about." Again, the blush I am not attempting to hide resurfaces. His finger moves from my lip, delicately trailing along my cheek, jaw, and neck.

"Like I said before, ask nicely before I let you feel the pleasure of my tongue."

Do I want that? I look at him and notice he does not have any glamor. He has two ivory horns curved on either side of his head, just above his pointed ears. But those are not the most notable features. It's his eyes. The deepest shade of blue, matching that of the Cerilian Sea.

I reach out and hesitantly touch his cheek. "Why?"

"Why what?" He asks.

"Why do I want you?" I whisper.

"Do you want me?" He asks as if he does not believe me and all the malicious thoughts, I had about seducing him are gone as I look at the real him. Something deep inside of me surfaces and I realize I do. "Answer me." He growls.

The intensity of his glare has my knees buckling and when I almost give into this urge, a knock sounds on the door, snapping me out of whatever trance I was in. "I guess you will never know."

I move to step out of the cage of his arms, but he grips my hips. "Where are you going?"

"To change." I shrug, as if his touch is not affecting me at all.

"Liar." He smirks and the knocking on his door increases. "We aren't done."

"I think we are." I stare him down and the person on the other side shouts.

"If you do not open this fucking door, I am going to blast it."

"Morgan," He growls. Who is that? His lover? Why do I even care? He is a shifter and my sworn enemy; regardless of the fact that he saved my life. "Stay in your room and don't come out until I come get you."

"I don't take orders from you, shifter boy." I look away and try to wiggle out of his grip. One hand loosens only to grab my chin and force my gaze back towards him.

"I'm not fucking around, princess. Do as I say or else."

"Or else what?" I square up to him and wait for an answer. Instead of answering me, he moves faster than I expect as I am lifted over his shoulder and carried to my room. "Let me go!"

The slap resounds as the palm of his hand lands on my ass cheek before he tosses me on the bed. He locks the door behind him. "Asshole."

Pressing my ear to the door, I hear distant murmurs. Looking back at the room, I decide to snoop. The dresser is first, only nothing is inside the four drawers. Moving to the closet, I notice there is also nothing inside. I sink to the floor, allowing myself a moment of self-pity. "Ugh! What kind of asshole doesn't have secrets?"

"The kind that doesn't appreciate nosy brats snooping through his things." I flinch at the sound of his deep voice. "And if I had any, why would they be in my guest bedroom?" He doesn't give me a chance to snap back. "Put these clothes on. We're leaving."

He tosses a pile at me before charging out of the room, leaving me dumbfounded on the carpeted floor.

ALEX

I stand at the end of the hallway, monitoring the time whilst waiting for her highness to come out as I look down at the text message my father sent me.

Sperm Donor:
Change of plans. There is a bounty for the Sagittarian Court's princess's head. I want it. If you do not deliver it to me by the end of the month, I will ensure you never breathe again.

Nothing more, nothing less. A simple order that I am expected to follow.

"What's that?" I quickly slip my phone into the jacket pocket of my black suit.. When my eyes land on her figure, my mouth dries and my cock stirs at the sight of her. Tight blue jeans hug the curves of her body perfectly. The pink tank top and leather jacket Morgan gave me leaves nothing to the imagination. "Hello?"

Clearing my throat, I handed over her newly repaired glasses and meet her curious eyes. "I got them fixed. Now you will not be so blind." I deadpan. She doesn't seem to understand my humor. "Come on, we need to leave."

I turn away from her , heading towards the front door. I do not look over my shoulder to see if she is following me, because I can sense it.

Walking down the steps to the ground floor, I think about

what my next move is going to be. Father wants her dead. I should be an obedient son and follow through, but I just cannot. There is something about her that makes me want to protect her from everything, including myself.

"Where are we going?" She speaks up for the first time since we left the apartment a few minutes ago, as we step onto the street that leads directly to one of my many casinos. "Why are you taking me into a bar?"

"It's not a bar, princess." I smirk as I grip the metal knob, open the side door, and walk in. The place is vacant of the usual customers, which is to be expected at this time of day. Cigarette smoke and alcohol cling to the air like a moth to a flame, despite the daily use of cleansing products.

Following the narrow hall that connects to the lobby, I nod a greeting to the cleaners as they sanitize the machines. The large space is filled with rows of slow machines, various card tables with the VIP game room at the very back. The bar is placed at the front and holds only top shelf liquor.

My office is on the top floor. I hear her soft steps follow me as we make our way up the spiraling metal staircase until stepping onto the plush black carpet of the viewing area. Before making it into the office, I turn back towards her and say, "Please do nothing stupid while I am at this meeting. Do not speak to anyone and do not leave this area."

She crosses her arms and raises her eyebrow at my

commands. My cock stirs with her unspoken defiance and the image of me bending her over that railing, spanking her ass raw, and fucking her into submission has me at full mast within seconds. "I'm serious, princess."

"Can I at least get a glass of whiskey?" She asks, and I note the annoyance in her tone. I dislike the idea of her drinking alone. Anyone could try to take advantage of her.

"No."

"You can't keep acting like my prison guard. I am a human being, for god's sake." She closes the few feet of distance in four strides. "Besides, I am leaving." She turns on her heel, but I snatch her by the back of her neck, wrapping an arm tightly around her waist, and growl.

"If you take one more step towards the stairs, I will bend you over that railing, tie your wrists behind your back, with your legs spread wide, and spank you for disobeying me." Her body shudders at my words and the scent of her arousal hits me, turning my cock to steel. "You're not in control here, princess."

"Get off me." It comes out breathlessly as she does not try to move away from me and we both know she could easily get out of my hold on her.

Leaning forward, I whisper against her ear. "Your words mean nothing when your body tells it all." I hum while running the tip of my nose along her neckline, breathing in her floral scent. She cranes her neck ever so slightly and I chuckle. "You're not a princess, no, you're my vixen."

"What does that mean?" She asks, and I catch onto the rise and fall of her chest.

"Be a good girl and I might reward you with an answer." I step away, leaving her breathless while I walk into my office, trusting her to stay put.

"What did I do to deserve a visit from my king?"

"Lettie." I say her name just as the door closes, and she turns around in the chair to face me. Her purple eyes lock onto me as she gives me a knowing smile. "By the look on your face, I'm sure you know why I am here."

"It is the young princess sitting outside this office." She claps her hands in front of her on the desk, her gray curls falling forward with the movement. I walk to the world map pinned to the side wall and admire it.

"For such a vast world, we know so little." Her shoulder brushes my elbow and I look down at her. "I am a dutiful son. I have been following his orders for the past thirty years."

"Is defying him worth the consequences? Is she worth it?"

Without hesitation, I answer, "Yes."

She cranes her neck to look up at me, "My dear boy, have you found your mate within the soul of a human?" Her violet eyes widen with curiosity. I rub my chin, unsure how to answer her and she must sense it, because what she says next baffles me even further. "Do not answer that question for my benefit. Either way, I will support whatever decision you choose to make."

"I'm delighted and humbled by your loyalty, but I came here because I suspect she is my mate. I do not know how that is possible. Shouldn't there be a zap of magic between us? What if she isn't my mate? And I am hesitant because I am lusting for her." She chuckles at my rambling. I never ramble. Gods help me.

"Come, sit. I will consult with the fates." I take a seat across from her while she pulls out her bag of miscellaneous items. Lettie is a witch amongst us shifters. I have known her my entire life. She was my mother's best friend, and despises my father with every fiber of her existence.

A large wooden bowl is placed on a black mat in the center of the desk. She scoops up some bones and recites an incantation I do not understand. Throwing the bones down in the bowl, she hovers her hands over them and translates their meaning. "Through blood and death, bones and shard, betrayal and lust, will your queen make herself known to you?"

"That's it? A fucking riddle?"

"Never curse the fates, boy." She looks back down at the mixture of bones, and I notice all the color drain from her face.

"What do you see?" She shakes her head. "Come on, tell me."

"Do you see this?" She points at two bones pointing in opposite directions of each other. "This means two paths. And this," she points at two bones forming what looks to be a heart, then on the other side, an X. "One path will lead you to your mate and the other to your death. Every choice you make from this moment forward will define your future, and hers."

"Should I tell her?" She sighs before standing and making her way to stand in front of me, cupping my cheek just like she did when I was a child.

"That is your choice." I sigh this time, welcoming her motherly touch, reminding me of when my mother would do comforting things such as these. "My dear boy, being an adult and a king means making tough decisions. But I know you will do whatever you think is right."

I open my eyes and kiss her palm before getting to my feet. "Thank you. I need to get going."

I take my leave, gripping the door handle, but pause when she speaks again. "When you are ready, I would like to meet her."

I smirk and leave, ensuring the door is closed before looking for my princess. When my eyes land on her looking out over the railing, I do not shy away from admiring her curves and ass.

"You have a fine establishment, shifter boy." I move closer to the space behind her. Gripping the railing on either side of her hips, caging her in my arms. "You don't have a clue what personal space is, do you?"

"Perhaps if you quit calling me boy, I wouldn't feel the need to remind you I am a man." I push my erection into her ass, and she gasps.

"Only, you're not a man." She turns around to face me. "You're a shifter. A cold-blooded killer. A Monster."

The last word is nothing but a whisper between us.

"Come, we are leaving." I step away from her before I lose control and show her what a monster I can be.

"Finally." She huffs as she follows me down the stairs. I smile to myself as we round the corner that leads down the hallway we came through when we got here, only to stop dead in my tracks at who was coming towards me. In a split second of panic, I wrench my arm backwards, snaring and squishing her between the wall and a slot machine. "What the?"

"Walton." I mutter and notice she has stopped squirming with the warning look I gave her.

"Alexxander." He says back to me.

"Why are you here?" I ask through bared teeth. He sticks his hands into the pockets of his yellow and purple pin-striped suit. The ugliest combination I have ever seen in my entire life.

"The king sent me to ensure you follow through on his last order." He states while leaning against the wall. His black hair is slicked back behind his pointed ears. My fingers itching with the need to blast him with a fireball. Walton is my father's advisor and in charge of all of us Mafia Dons. It makes me sick to my stomach knowing all the immoral things this scum has done. I suppose that is why father made him second in command.

"It will be done. I already have my men searching for her at this very moment." He gives me an effortless smirk.

"Come now, Bowie, last I heard, she was seen entering this casino about an hour ago." I cringe at the sound of the nickname he gave me as an insult.

"Your reports are wrong. If she were in my casino, I would know it." I catch movement out of the corner of my eye. I do not react as to not give away anything to Walton. If he finds her alive and, in my casino, all hell will break loose.

"Then you wouldn't mind if me and my men look around."

"Be my guests, but if anyone destroys anything or harasses my staff, I will kill them." I warn and he chuckles, a deep one from within his black soul. While they move forward, I step backwards, taking a quick glance at the spot I put her. Panic seizes as I see she's gone.

Always, the defiant one.

CHAPTER 6

GWEN

BREATHE GWEN, BREATHE.

As soon as I heard the bastard speak the word her I took my life into my own hands and took off. Well, more like crawling off, which I only regret as my palms press onto the sticky surface of the floor, but I ignore it, swallowing the bile in my throat.

I make my way past the slot machines lining the back wall, monitoring the people walking around the other side. I stop at the gap between the wall I am using as my anchor, and the front door. Freedom is right there; I only must ensure that no one sees me as I run across the open hallway and out the door.

You are a fucking warrior. Get your shit together. I am no man's prisoner. Peeking my head out, I look left, then right and once more before making a break for it.

"She's escaping." I hear someone yell as I throw the door

open and run out into the brisk afternoon air. Pumping my arms, I sprint down the street, looking for a place I could use as sanctuary, only to come up short. Anyone caught harboring me would meet the same fate, and I cannot let that happen.

Zig zagging down street after street, I do not stop until I know I have lost my followers. Without looking behind me, I press my back to the wall of a building to catch my breath.

"I think she went this way." Shit. I slink down and crawl behind some bushes, making my body flush with the ground. I reach for the dagger in my right boot, holding it at the ready in case I need to use it.

"I think you look rather delectable on your back." Alex's voice reaches me just as he looks down at me. Jumping to my feet, I ready my stance as my blade is clutched tightly in my fist.

"Get away from me." I growl and he sighs, shaking his head.

"I will not hurt you."

"I don't believe you." He sighs again, stuffing his hands in his pockets and leaning against a post.

"Look, if I wanted to hurt you, I could."

"I'd like to see you try." I bare my teeth, not lowering my arms in case this is a trick. He takes one hand out of his pocket and rubs his chin.

"As tempting as that is, I think we should get you somewhere safe."

"I'm not going anywhere with you. I heard what that man said. You have orders to kill, and I assume the her he was talking about is me."

"I told you I would take you to your friends. I am still willing to help you, but you must trust me."

"Never. I do not need you or anyone trying to take care of me. I've been doing that for twenty-four years." He closes the distance between us, and I place my dagger against his throat, while my free hand rears back into a punch.

"Do you wish to kill me?" His eyes are hooded with desire. I swallow the lump forming in my throat as I stare at him. He reaches out with one hand, gripping my throat softly. His thumb runs up and down the side of it and I get lost in the heat of the moment.

"What are you doing?" I ask myself more than him as I shake my head and press the dagger against him, walking him backwards until he is pressed against the wall. "I'm going to walk away. If you follow me, try to stop me, or make any attempts to touch me, I will not hesitate."

"One of these days, you will learn to trust me."

"Never." I back away from him until I am a good enough distance and take off in a sprint, dagger out and at the ready.

Night falls as the moon rises and my feet have formed blisters on them. I find myself at the edge of Rose City. Crossing a bridge over a small stream, I make my way into Kalice City, where I am sure no one will know who I am and have one goal in mind-find a bed and a phone.

As I make my way through the quiet street, I sigh with relief at the sign labeled Cottonwood Inn and an arrow pointing to the fifth building down the right side. Walking up the five stone steps, I tuck my dagger away before gripping the golden knob and pushing the wooden door open. The warming scent of apple pie fills the lobby and makes me smile.

A woman sits behind a counter made of oak, typing away at her computer. Walking up, I wait for her to acknowledge me. When she does not, I go to speak, but she holds up a finger. "I'll be with you in just a moment, my dear. Have a slice of pie. I made it myself."

I look over at the encased pie, and my stomach growls as my mouth waters.

Picking up the plate, I lift the glass top off the case, cut myself a piece, and place it on my plate. Grabbing a fork, I cut off a piece and plop it into my mouth. Cinnamon and apple send my taste buds into overdrive as I practically moan with the flavor. The crust is buttery and compliments the fruity flavor perfectly. "This is orgasmic."

"Beg pardon?" Her cheeks flush.

"Sorry, it's delicious." She smirks at me, and I set the plate down.

"One room?" She asks.

"Yes, and I would like to use your phone, please."

"We don't have one."

"What? How?"

She chuckles while getting a key from the drawer in front of her. "We do not have the funding."

That is news to me. "Surely you've contacted the mayor." She sighs as she hands me the key.

"We have, but the Lord Regent and Princess have made it known that the money is being put to use elsewhere." That really is news to me.

"Where?"

"Rumor is, it's for the army." I raise a brow, not wanting to believe her. "Apparently, the dragon shifters are planning to invade again. After twenty years, you'd think a magical wall would keep them out."

"I assure you that there is no war."

"How can you be sure? Do you work at the palace?" I stop myself, remembering I need to stay incognito.

"No."

"Then how could you possibly know?" an awkward silence brews between us, only interrupted by the front door opening and my current confusion, turns to blistering rage at who comes walking in with his glamor intact, looking all god-like. My core clenches at the sight of him, and I look away.

"Hello, darling. Is the room ready for us?"

"Oh, is this your husband?" The woman blushes and I roll my eyes.

"We are on our honeymoon." He boasts and grips my shoulders, and because my body hates me, instead of it retracting like any normal person would, my skin heats and I rub my thighs together as my pussy throbs.

"Congratulations. Why didn't you say something, dear? I have the perfect room for you."

"It's unnecessary." I say, trying to hide my annoyance, but he takes the new key and I reluctantly hand her back the first one.

"It's the only room on the third floor. Completely private." She smirks, and I turn to leave.

"Thank you." I hear him state and I make my way up the stairs, not caring if he is following me or not. Once outside the door, I gag at the golden heart welded around the peephole.

"Allow me." I step aside as he unlocks the door and I push

past him to get inside.

The walls are pure white, with a king-sized mattress covered in crimson sheets at the center. A single ivory oak wardrobe sits next to the door. I can only assume leads into the bathroom, and two end tables that match the wardrobe sit on either side of the headboard.

I hear the bedroom door close and lock. Turning, I charge at Alex, pulling my dagger that I hid within my jacket sleeve and swipe down, aiming for his heart. I am quick, but he is faster as he grips my wrist, spinning me around until my back hits the wall with a loud crack. His forearm presses into my chest as his knees push my legs apart, making it impossible for me to fight back.

"Easy, princess. Why don't we just talk about this?"

"I told you what would happen if you followed me." I spit at him while trying to wrench my dagger hand free. My other hand is pinned between my ass and the wall. I have no clue how he managed that.

"And I told you, you could trust me." He growls.

"I don't give a fuck what you have to say. All that has ever come out of your mouth are lies."

"No, princess, I have not and never will lie to you. I may have withheld some minor details, but I was hoping to see you safe before having to tell you." I move to stab him again, but he adds pressure, making me wince. "I don't want to hurt you. I'm going to step back, but if you try to stab me again, I will ensure you are tied to each bedpost with a gag in your mouth while I talk to you."

Gods, I hate this man and his dirty mouth. Yeah, sure you do.

He steps back, putting distance between us. I think about

attacking just to see if he would go through with his threat but think better of it. Placing my dagger inside my boot, I fold my arms and raise a brow. "Speak."

"There is a bounty on your head." When he waits to see I give no fucks, he continues. "My father ordered me to bring him your head."

"And?" I angle my hip and begin tapping my foot.

"And I am disobeying him. What more do you want from me, princess?"

"I want you to leave." I point to the door, and he scoffs while shaking his head.

"You're so infuriating. Did you not hear what I just said?"

"Yeah, so? Why should I care? I am a princess; royals get threats all the time." He stalks closer to me, but I do not back away.

"You're clearly not getting it. A bounty has been placed on you. Which means every cutthroat criminal in this entire world is looking to make a quick buck. You have a target on your pretty little head and if I am caught helping you, I will have a target as well." I laugh at the ultimate admission I was waiting for. "You think this is funny?"

"No. Now get out." I stand my ground against him. Although he has his glamor up, I can still see the dark shades behind the light in his human-like eyes.

"All I am trying to do is protect you."

"No, you're trying to protect yourself."

He tosses his hands up and turns away.

"You know, when Walton came inside to find you, I could've easily handed you over to him." He scrubs his face before looking at me. "I don't care if I live or die. I just care about doing what's right, and if you can't see that, then I truly am wasting my time." The truth and pleading in his eyes has me questioning my doubt.

"Do you know who placed the bounty on my head?"

"Yes." I wait for him to answer, praying it is not someone I know. "Prince Mauris of the Lirian Court and," he pauses a moment. "Your Lord Regent."

I knew the Lord Regent was an ass, but a traitor? "How do you know?" I need proof beyond reasonable doubt.

"The day of your ball, they came to proposition me in my office."

"Unbelievable." I scoff, tossing my hands into the air.

"I didn't go through with it, obviously." He makes a pointed gesture at me and my still intact body.

"Yet you showed up at the ball."

"And it's a good thing I did or else you would be six feet under." We are a breath apart from each other and I do not know if I want to slap him or kiss him. I will not allow myself to do either. I take a step back, and keep moving until I am pressed against the wall again.

"We're done here. You need to leave." He walks towards me and veers off at the last second, gripping the handle. I see him pull something from his jacket pocket.

"For you to contact your friends... and me." Before I can respond, he places the phone on the wardrobe and leaves. Regret consumes me, but I shove it off just as quickly as it comes and grab the phone before making my way into the bathroom, shutting and locking the door.

I look down and notice only one contact listed under the name Shifter Boy, and I do not fight the smirk that spreads across my face. I pull up the dial pad and punch in Tori's number.

"Hello?" My heart jumps with glee at the sound of her voice.

"Tori, it's me."

"Gwen? What? Where are you and whose phone are you using?" She sounds groggy, as if I just woke her up.

"None of that matters. Are you and Diliha okay?" I hear some shuffling in the background, not sure what it is before she answers.

"Gwen," Diliha's voice comes through and a tear escapes at the relief I feel, knowing my best friends are safe and together.

"Yeah, girl, it's me." The tears fall. "I miss you both so much."

"It's been twenty-four hours." Tori states.

"I know, but still." I hold back from completely breaking down.

"Gwen, what happened?" Diliha's sweet voice almost brings me to my knees. I know I cannot tell them or else they will be in danger. Which also means I cannot go to them.

"Nothing. I just needed to get away for a while. I forgot my phone, so I bought this new one." I answer.

"You sound upset. Why don't you tell us where you are so we can be with you?" Tori asks, and my heart hurts from lying to them.

"No. I don't want anyone to know. Otherwise, Lord Pervert might force me to come back." I feign a laugh, but I can tell by the silence on the other end they do not believe me.

"Whatever it is you are going through, we are just glad you are safe and alive." Tori says after a while.

"There was a dead shifter found right outside the ballroom." She states.

"Blood was everywhere. It looked like someone literally

ripped his throat out." Diliha inputs and I instantly think of Alex.

"A shifter? Are you sure?" I ask.

"He had horns and everything. It was the guy that was dancing with you before you left. Only we think he was using a glamor. Oh, and Prince Mauris and the Lord Regent are missing." She adds, and I hear Tori hiss at her.

"Missing? They never showed up?" I ask, disbelieving.

"No, and one more thing," Tori adds, and I am not sure I can handle much more. "Another war is brewing."

"Fuck. All right, look, I got to go but I will talk soon. Don't give this number to anyone and don't tell anyone you talked to me." I order them.

"Okay, we love you. If you need us, just call." Tori murmurs and we end the call. I called Alex, to get a handle on this missing person's thing.

"Miss me already, princess?" He smugly taunts, his deep voice vibrating through the phone directly to my core. Ignoring my raging hormones, I answer him.

"Never. What did you do to Mauris and the Regent?" I ask, cutting straight to the point.

"Nothing." He answers curtly.

"You said they propositioned you before the ball. They never showed up. Oh, and what about this dead shifter at the ball?" I ask, doing my best to sound pissed.

"He hurt you." He growls.

"So, you killed him?"

"He deserved to die for hurting you." There was no hint of sarcasm or humor, and I do not know how to feel about this. "As for the other two, I had their memories swiped and then released them. Whatever happened to them afterwards is not on me."

"You truly are an ass." He chuckles and I realize I love hearing that sound. Silence develops between us, and I blush.

"Is there anything else?" He asks in a seductive tone.

"Thank you."

"For?" I roll my eyes, picturing the smirk on his face.

"For saving my life and giving me this phone." I spit out fast.

"I will always protect you, princess." My heart flutters at his words. I shut that shit down quickly, not knowing what that was about.

"Stop that." I berate him.

"Stop what?

"Saying things." I sigh.

"What frightens you most, my words as a man, or that I am a shifter?" I do not have to think because I already know the answer.

"Both." I end the call before the conversation continues and silence the ringer before putting it face down and turning towards the shower.

After getting undressed, I hop into the warm spray and sit on the tiled floor. My tears mixed with the water as I let go of everything I have been holding back since I was attacked. I place my head face down and close my eyes, clearing my mind as I try to think of a plan.

The first part is a new disguise. Part two: new clothes. The safe house is part three. Part four, who am I kidding? I need money for all this. And help. Getting to my feet, I wash the day away before getting out to dry off. Noticing I do not have any other clothes, I put the complimentary bathrobe on and head to the room.

The bathrobe is what I imagine being wrapped up in a fluffy cloud would feel like. Soft with the smell of fresh linen. I sit on the bed, and sigh before looking at my phone screen.

Shifter Boy:
Dream of me tonight, princess.

Me:
Not a chance.

Shifter Boy:
What are you doing still awake?

Me:
Shower first, then sleep

Shifter Boy:
You are naked and wet. I will use that delectable image later (wink emoji)

I blush and giggle, then do something I never thought I would. I part the robe just enough to show off my cleavage, sit up on my knees, and take a picture.

Shifter Boy:
Are you trying to kill me, princess?

Me:
Always.

I wait for him to respond but when it shows read and nothing else; I sigh and put the phone down, tucking myself into the throes of the comforter before drifting off into the wonderful world of dreams.

ALEX

I never really left the inn.

My room sits directly below Gwen's to ensure she's safe throughout the night. I did not expect her to reply to my message and when she did; I sat up and engaged. The last message surprised me the most and all my control went out the window.

Ensuring my glamor is up, I grab my suit jacket, jerk the door open, and rush up the stairs. I raise my hand to knock, but stop myself. We cannot go there. Not with her, not right now.

Knocking on her door, I impatiently wait for her to open it, but I know she is there. I can sense her on the other side.

"Princess?" I ask. When I am about to give up and retreat, the door opens, and I lose myself at the sight of her in that tight bathrobe.

"What are you doing here?" She asks. I stride into the room, forcing her to stumble back a step before I turn to lock the door. I stand for a moment, letting my hands rest against the warn wood as my back remains to her. *What am I doing?*

"Why are you here?"

I clench my fingers, trying to contain myself before I move too fast. Then decide, fuck it, and go for it. Turning, I move without thinking and crash my lips to hers. When she does not pull away or kiss me back, I break away. I stare into her eyes to read her emotions. "I just needed to say goodnight."

"Goodnight." She whispers back while I run my thumb up and down her cheek. "Would you like to stay with me?"

"If I stay with you in that bed, we will do anything but sleep." She bites her lip, which has my cock jumping to attention.

"Like what?" She asks. I could die from the temptation of her. The scent of her arousal calling me.

"Don't ask questions you don't really want to know the answer to." I warn her.

"Maybe I want you to show me." I groan as she reaches out to touch my face. "Maybe I want to cross that line tonight."

"Don't play with me, princess. Tell me what you want, and I will give it to you."

"I want release. I want a distraction from everything that is going on outside these four walls."

"Are you sure?" I need her consent.

"Yes."

"Get on the bed."

She hesitates but does what I say, making my self-control teeter. Taking my suit jacket off, I toss it on the floor before stepping up to her. "Give me the sash, turn around, and put your hands behind your back."

She complies and I tie the sash around her wrist, ensuring it is tight enough she won't move, but not tight enough to hurt her. Placing myself behind her, I get the consent I need before moving any further. "I'm going to fuck your tight little cunt, princess. But first, I'm going to punish you for baiting me." She gasps. "If this is not what you want, then tell me."

She turns her head to look at me. "I need it."

She Pauses.

"Tell me." I cup the side of her cheek.

"I need release."

"Do you want me to fuck you?" She nods, "Use your words princess."

"I want you to fuck me."

I groan and crush my lips to hers. Sticking my tongue into her mouth as she is kissing me back with just as much force. "Alex," she says, and I love hearing my name on her lips. "If you're going to fuck me, then fuck me as the monster you are."

I groan as I let my glamor fall and I see her lust filled eyes gleam with the flush rising in her cheeks. "Any more requests, princess?" She shakes her head. I begin by elongating a talon, running it along her cheek, down her neck, and around her exposed breast.

"This robe." I hook the back of it and tear it from her body. "Needs to go."

I move behind her to get a view of her perfect ass. I push her forward, so her face is on the mattress and get a perfect view of her glistening pussy. Retracting my talon, I run my fingers through her folds. "Already so wet for me."

I pull the belt from my pants, "I'm going to punish you for tormenting me. Do you understand?"

"Yes." She breathes.

"If you take it like the good girl I know you are, I will reward you." I smack the belt across both cheeks, hard enough to leave a mark. I look at the wetness dripping from her pussy. I smack her twice more before I cannot hold back any longer.

Running my tongue through her folds, she jolts at the sudden feeling. I hold her still by gripping her wrists and pinning her in place. "You taste fucking delicious."

"Please." She begs.

"Already so close. But you cannot cum until I tell you to." I lick straight up her center, using my other hand to tease her clit.

"Fuck." She moans, wiggling as I press two fingers inside her finding the perfect rhythm between my mouth and my fingers. "Please, I'm so close."

"Not yet." When I know she is about to tip over, I pull back and chuckle at the frustrated groan.

"Finish me or I will do it myself." She growls and I cup her pussy.

"This pussy belongs to me." I state.

"Prove it." She retorts and I push my fingers inside her while biting her clit. She screams as her release hits her hard. I continue to lick her through it. When she is done, I step back and pull all my clothes off. Gripping my cock, I run my hand up and down it while I position myself on the bed behind her. "Wait."

"Okay." I choke out.

"Untie me. I need to touch you." I have had no one touch me before.

"I can't." I look away in shame. "Something happened in my past. I'd rather not discuss it."

"Then this goes no further." I know she is being stern, and my cock wants to protest, but I untie her bindings and move to get dressed. "You don't have to get dressed."

"If we are both naked, I'm going to fuck you." I do not look at her as I pull my boxers on.

"At least let me help you." I turn around and see her on her knees before me. Holy fucking goddess.

"Are you sure?" I ask, and she reaches out to pull my boxers down. I step out of them, and she looks at me with hooded eyes.

"I'm going to touch you." I nod and when her hand wraps around my shaft, I shudder at her touch, leaning into it. "Tell me what to do." She likes me to be in control.

"Lick the tip while pumping me." When her tongue does

just that, I wrap her hair around my hand. "Again." She repeats it. "Take me as deep as you can, then swallow." I groan as she does it. "So, fucking perfect."

"Fuck my mouth." She asks as she licks the pre-cum from my tip. She does not have to ask me twice to thrust back in and pick the rhythm I want. I look deep into her eyes, watching as the tears fall, but she never tells me to stop.

"You're mine." I growl as I fuck her tight mouth. "No one will ever be allowed to touch you again." She moans against my cock. "Touch yourself." I see her hand move to her pussy as she finger fucks herself. "So fucking perfect, taking my cock like the queen you are."

I fuck her hard and fasts, not as fast if it were her pussy, but she takes it. When she makes herself cum, I groan at the pure beauty of it. "I could watch you cum all day." She reaches up with the fingers she just fucked herself with and reaches behind me. I am too caught up in her mouth. I do not know what she is doing until her fingers thrust into my ass. I cum instantly.

"Fuck, princess." I hold her still until she swallows all my seed. I pull her to her feet and crush my mouth to hers. Tasting myself on her tongue. Her nails wrack down my back and I walk her backwards until her knees hit the bed. She falls backwards and I hover over her as I kiss her again. This time slower.

"Alex," she breaks our kiss and I look for any sign of regret. She places a hand on my cheek, her eyes move to my ears, as her hand follows the path until she touches my horns. I groan. "Did I hurt you?"

"They're sensitive, princess. And I suggest if you do not want to fuck, stop touching them." She does not move her hand immediately and I harden again.

"Not tonight." She speaks. "Especially if I can't touch you. I will not ask why, but until you are ready. This is all we'll ever do." She kisses me softly, and I press my forehead to hers. "You can sleep here if you wish. But I need to pee." I roll off her and allow her to do her thing.

You are an idiot. My inner dragon berates me for not succumbing to the need to stake a claim on her pussy, but I cannot give her what she wants. Not yet. When my eyes close, I do not open them until I feel her head laying on my chest and her fingers running through my chest hair.

"Do you regret it?" I ask, knowing how she feels about shifters.

"No. But," she props herself on her elbow and I turn on my side so I can face her. "I need to figure out what to do from here. I can't exactly live on the run."

"You can stay with me." She smiles and I like that reaction rather than her trying to kill me.

"No, that was a onetime thing."

I growl and move over her. "This pussy belongs to me." I cup her still wet sex and she arches into my touch. I thrust two fingers inside her while my thumb circles her clit.

"Alex," she moans.

"Tell me who this pussy belongs to, and I will let you cum." I growl, waiting for her to answer me.

"You."

"Who?"

"My pussy belongs to you, Alex." I groan and crush my lips against her until she is moaning, and her pussy is clenching around my fingers. I pull my fingers out of her pussy and raise them to her mouth. "Taste yourself."

She wraps her lips around my fingers and sucks. "Good girl. Now about this plan."

"Fucking hell, shifter boy. What a way to ruin shit." I chuckle at her and she wiggles beneath me. We both freeze as the tip of my cock brushes against her entrance. I quickly get off her and move to grab my boxers. "We can talk about that tomorrow."

"Hmm. First, I'm going to kill everyone who has ever threatened you. Then I will help you get your place upon the throne."

"Seriously?" She asks incredulously as I make my way back to the bed, lifting the covers to getting under them. She mimics my move but doesn't come any closer.

"I'll figure out where Mauris and the Regent went. We'll start with them and make our way through the city until we can figure out what is going on."

"What did the Lord Regent tell you when he asked you to kill me?" I turn over and face her.

"Mauris wants you dead because he blames your father for the death of all the monarch's parents."

"Never. They were killed by shifters."

"No, princess, they weren't."

"How?" She cups her mouth.

"I used a memory potion on a witness, and it played out the events of the day. Your father gave them all poisoned wine. It looked like your mother was already dead." She sits up with her hand over her heart and I rub a hand down her back.

"And Warren?" She looks at me with glossed over eyes.

"He just wants your throne."

"Right. Fuck."

I sit up to move behind her. Wrapping my arms around her

as I let her lean on me.

"I'm sorry, princess. I thought you knew. Is that why you hate my kind?" I keep rubbing a soothing hand down her back, and she leans against me.

"Yes. I was told shifters killed all the monarchs because King Outher wanted to enslave us all. Do you know him?"

My hand stops as I contemplate my answer, "He's my father."

She snaps her head to look at me. "Wait, you're the son of the Dragon King? That means you're a prince."

I shrug. "Titles don't mean shit to me."

"But you're also the Mafia King of the city." I cock a brow at her. "I looked up shifters that match your name."

"What does the Iticha web disclose about me?" I genuinely want to know because that is a security hazard.

"Nothing. It just says Alex: Mafia King of Sagittarian Court."

"When did you do this?" I ask.

"While I took my piss." She admits.

"How? You were in the bathroom for like two seconds." She leans forward and kisses my nose.

"Never underestimate a woman. We surprise you." I grip her hips and spin her, so she is straddling me.

"Don't I know it?" I kiss her and groan as her arousal soaks the fabric of my boxers, making me hard again.

"Fuck me." She whispers against my lips as her hands go to my waistband. "I won't touch you. I need you inside me."

"No." She stops. "I want to give you everything. I just can't, not right now." She sighs when I cup her cheek.

"Okay. But... I need to ask you something."

"I'm an open book, princess."

"What's going to happen when this is all over? When I take back my throne and we kill everyone who has threatened me?" I know what she wants me to say, but I would never be accepted by her side.

"You will become Queen and I will go back to doing what I do best. Ridding this world of all the criminals. Protecting the innocent while maintaining a business." She sighs.

"Good thing we have no chance of falling in love with each other." She jokes, but I can hear the sadness in her voice.

"Yeah." I sigh as she nuzzles into my hold and soon she falls asleep. I look at her flawless beauty and something snaps inside of me. My eyes close and I face my inner beasts for the first time in a long time.

"*Our mate.*" The golden dragon speaks into the darkness of my mind. "*Princess Gwen of the Sagittarian Court is our mate. We shall protect her with our life.*"

"She is a human. How can this be?"

"*Only the fates decide who our mate is. Human or not, she is ours. Solidify the bond before the next full moon or she will be lost to us forever.*"

"I won't force her."

"*I know.*" I am whisked back to reality and look back down at her. And whisper against her lips. "My mate. My princess. I will protect you with my life until the end of time." I kiss her and then settle into a deep sleep with my arm around her.

CHAPTER 7

GWEN

MY EYES FLUTTER OPEN and I reach for him, only to find the bed is empty on his side. *Was it all a dream?* I look around, my gaze landing on the torn robe and smile. It certainly *wasn't* a dream. Tossing the sheets off me, I make my way to the bathroom to pee and shower.

The warm water flows down my front as I close my eyes and feel relaxed for the first time since I could remember. I jump as firm hands move around my waist, and a warm chest presses flush against my back. "Did you sleep well, princess?"

"Very." I turn around, opening my eyes, but not before he kisses me. I look into his blue eyes and never want to get lost in any other man's gaze. It scares me, because I know that this will never go beyond what happened in this hotel room. Whatever we have is forbidden.

"What are you thinking about?" He whispers against my

lips.

"How I never want to leave this room." I answer honestly, and he presses his forehead to mine.

"I know." We stay like that for a while. Savoring the moment before, we must step back into the real world. "We should go."

"One more minute won't hurt." I kiss him, and he deepens it, pushing his tongue forward and lifting me up. I wrap my legs around his waist and moan at the feeling of his cock brushing against me. He is hesitant when he lets me touch him.

"Princess," he warns.

"Don't you want me?" I ask, hating the desperation that comes out with the words.

"More than anything."

"Something happened to you." He says nothing, just nods in response and looks away. I grip his chin the way he does me and turn his face to look at me. "When you're ready, I'll be here."

He kisses me intensely once more before setting me down and walking out. I finish washing myself before getting out and drying off. "Have you seen my clothes?"

"In here, princess." I walk into the bedroom to see a new outfit laid on the bed.

"You went shopping?" I pick up the pink top and black jeans, then eye the red laced panty and bra set. "In the women's section."

"No, Morgan did." There is that name again.

"And who's that?" I ask while pulling on the bra and panties. Hating the idea of this Morgan picking out my clothes.

"My general." He states as I pull the pants on next, then the top, finishing the outfit with new socks, my boots, and the leather jacket. I turn around and he captures my chin, kissing me again. "And my sister."

"Oh." I say and he smiles.

"Come on, princess. Let's get you fed." I smile as we interlace our fingers and he glamor's himself. We exit the room and make our way down the stairs. The smell of bacon makes my stomach growl with hunger as we stroll through the lobby into the dining area.

I fill my plate with fruit and bacon before taking a seat at the far back right. Alex follows suit, only he has two cups of coffee and nothing else. "You're not hungry?"

"Not a breakfast person." He sips on his coffee while I eat my strawberries and think of what we will do next.

"Are we going back to your apartment?" He looks around, as if scanning for threats, although we are the only ones in here besides the kitchen staff.

"No. That has been compromised." I sip on my coffee, surprised that he got the sugar to caffeine ratio correct, while he continues to look around. Abruptly, he gets to his feet. "Stay here and do not move until I come back for you."

"What's going on?" I get to my feet.

"Please listen to me." I nod and he closes the pocket doors, leaving me alone with the person refilling the eggs. I finish my breakfast while I continue to wait. Pulling out my phone, I notice I have a message from Tori and Diliha. They have created a group chat.

Tori:
Is this true?

Diliha:
Are you with a Mafia Shifter?

I click on the article and read the headline Sagittarian Court's very own Princess, getting cozy with the infamous Mafia King. And then I see the image. Someone snapped a picture of me and Alex in a very compromising position. He is in his shifter form, pressing me against the wall. I had my dagger to him, but from the angle you would never see it.

Tori:

Gwen, please answer us before I send my army across the border to rescue you.

Me:

It is not like the picture shows.

Diliha:

Tell us everything

Me:

I will call you later. XOXO

I click my phone off and make my way towards the pocket doors. Too much time has passed and if they saw this article, that means everyone with access to the world wide web does. Putting my phone in my jacket pocket, I pull the dagger from my boots and slide the doors open.

Looking around, I try to see if anyone is here. When I do not, my gut clenches. Something is very wrong. I walk past the desk and staircase, looking side to side. Another hallway is on the other side of the wall that connects to the stairs. I peek around to find a door at the very back.

I get my dagger at the ready and pause outside the door, keeping my steps as quiet as possible, while ensuring that my boots cannot be seen if they look under the door.

"Where's the princess?" It is that same guy, Walton, from the casino.

"I don't know." Alex answers and I hear something that sounds like a punch and Alex's deep laugh. "You'll have to do better than that."

"Are you willing to die for a worthless human?" He sneers and I can practically see the grimace on the shifter's face.

"She's worth more to me than all the gold in existence." My heart flutters at his declaration and a potent mixture of emotion overcomes me. Rage. I grab onto it and allow it to fill my entire body. Rushing through the door, all I see is red.

"Get the fuck away from him." I growl.

"Princess Gwen, welcome. We were just talking about you." Walton states as he points a dagger at Alex's chest. I eye it and he chuckles. "Oh, I see you know what this is."

"Shifter blade." I answer. A black iron-clad dagger infused with dragon blood.

"So, you know that if you make a wrong move, I will kill him."

"He is your king's son; I highly doubt that." The man chuckles.

"Outher? He cares about nothing but power. He'd be happy to be rid of this pathetic waste of space." With that statement, I move without thinking and slice the neck of the first person I come across. Blood splatters over me as I move forward and thrusts my blade into the chest of another. Spinning, I move toward another of the men, only stopping when I see the dagger being held against Alex's throat.

"Stop or I will kill him." Walton warns.

"Never." I snarl.

"Tell her boy. Once I kill you, she will be next." He warns, and Alex looks at me with pleading eyes. All I see is the blood seeping out from wounds along his face. One of his horns is cracked and there is a piece of flesh missing from his right ear.

"Princess, go." I look at his eyes again, then back at Walton.

"If I go with you, will you give me your word you will let him go?" I do not intend on leaving him with this cock sucker. I just need him to move Alex slightly further to the right. He chuckles.

"I can't believe this. A human and a shifter. Both royal and completely smitten with each other. You realize that it will never work, right? A union like this is forbidden."

"Are you going to answer the question or not?" I growl.

"Fine. I'll give you my word." My world slows down just as he drops the dagger. The dagger leaves my hand before he realizes what is happening. He falls to the floor, dead, with my knife between his eyes.

"What the fuck, princess?" He baulks as I rush over to him, cutting his bindings with Walton's blade, and help him to his feet. "You just killed him."

"Yeah. We need to leave." I mutter.

"They've seen us together in your shifter form. Is there anyone you can trust?" I ask while assessing his injuries.

"Only one. But then we are talking about what you just did." He states, and I roll my eyes.

"You act like you've never seen a woman who can throw knives."

"Not like that. I mean, Morgan can do a lot of things, but what you did takes pure fucking talent. And you know what else?" We hobble forward.

"What?"

"I'm so fucking turned on right now." My eyes travel to his crotch.

"Come on, shifter boy, can't you heal yourself so we can get out of here? Your kind of too heavy for me to carry."

"Kiss me." His words make me freeze for a moment.

"Really? You think now is the best time for this?"

"Just shut up and kiss me." He pleads. I sigh and cup his face, kissing him passionately. His arms wrap around me as he deepens it. I open my eyes and gasp at his healed face.

"How?" His brows furrow, and he evades the question by pulling me along behind him. I do not press any further as we make our way out of the Inn and onto the busy street. "How are we getting out of here?"

He turns to me, a smirk spreading across his face. "Do you trust me?" He reaches out a hand to me and I eye it suspiciously.

"No." I answer, but take his hand anyway. "But you're all I got." He pulls me against him, his human glamor completely gone.

"Hold on to me." Before I could ask why, we shoot off the ground as beautiful golden wings burst from his back. I look around and grip him tighter as I see the city far below us. "Look at me."

"Why didn't you think of this sooner?" I ask while looking into his eyes.

"Because I rarely fly." He shrugs as we soar through the skies.

"When was the last time you fully shifted?"

He looks away before answering, "The day my mom died." There is sorrow in his voice, and I cannot help the tear that falls for his pain. "Don't cry for me, princess. It was twenty years ago."

"How?" I ask, because despite myself, I am enjoying getting to know the man behind the beast.

"When I was ten years old, my dragon fully emerged. She was so proud of me, and we flew together. Father told us to never fly beyond the wall, but I wanted to see what humans looked like, and I figured they would never see us from way up here. I begged her to fly over, and she agreed because the moon was rising." He pauses a moment. "She was killed by a human the moment we passed over. A shifter arrow straight through the heart."

"Alex," A tear slips free from his right eye, and I wipe it away like he did for me.

"It's my fault and my father blamed me for it when I walked through the throne hall doors with her lifeless body in my arms. Every day, he beat me until I became submissive. But that wasn't the worst part." I do not know what to say or do, so I just lean my forehead to his, giving him all the strength I can. "On my eighteenth birthday, he told me it was time for me to become a man. He had five female human slaves naked in my bedroom. When I refused, he ordered the guards to bind my hands and ankles to the bedpost. And then, one by one, they used me for their pleasure."

I finally understand why he cannot face me. "I'll kill him for making you go through that."

"No, you won't, because that is what I am going to do." I kiss him, pouring all my strength into him. A warm feeling deep in my core fuels me from within. "Princess what, what are you doing?"

I open my eyes and see a glow on my hands, but it fades just as fast. "I was kissing you."

"But your hands." His brows are furrowed, but I shrug it off. Because glowing hands are meant for people with magic. Which means it was just a figment of my imagination. Being around him and his magical abilities must be screwing with my head.

"Must be the sun. Are we almost there?" I ask, he nods.

"I've never spoken to anyone about that since it all happened." He mutters after a short while.

"I will never tell another soul." I reassure him, gripping him tighter as we continue to speed through the air.

A few minutes later, we land on a metal rooftop somewhere in the middle of another city, and he snaps his wings back into place within his skin. He interlocks his fingers with mine as we walk to the edge of the building where he leans over and hops onto a patio, holding out his hands for me to jump into them.

I take my second leap of faith, and he catches me before setting me on the solid balcony. He reaches for the door, only to find it locked. "We'll have to wait until she comes here."

"Move over, shifter boy." I push him aside, pulling the pin from my hair before getting to work picking the lock. When the door lock clicks, I hear him whistle behind me.

"What other secret skills do you have?"

"Stick around and you might just find out." I wink before pushing the door in and stepping onto the ivory tile floor of the apartment. Alex closes the door, turning the lock, we make our way towards the couch sitting at the center of the open floor plan.

"We should be safe here for now." He states while wrapping an arm around me.

"What should we do now?" I ask.

"I have a few ideas." He smirks and kisses me, pushing me down onto my back.

"Oh, for goodness' sake, if you're sneaking your latest conquest into my apartment, send me a warning text. Why don't 'ya?" A woman's voice cuts through our growing tension and Alex moves off me.

"Morgan." He smiles and embraces a short shifter with pink pixie cut hair. I stand up and look at her while she steps away from her brother. She eyes me up and down before thrusting a punch into his arm. "What the fuck was that for?"

"For not calling me sooner, dipshit. With the entire world seeing you two all cozy, you should have called me. Why didn't you tell me about the damn princess? Wait, was she the one back in your apartment?" I hate it when people talk about me as if I am not in the room.

"That would be me." I say with a soft smile. She hits him again.

"That's for lying to me. What'd you think, I was going to betray you or something?" She scolds him and I burst out laughing.

"If I told you I was protecting the human princess, what would you have done?" She does not even hesitate to answer.

"I would've helped you with no questions asked. But now that I see her. I understand why you wanted her all to yourself." I hear a protective growl rumble in his throat.

"Watch how you speak about her."

"Easy, just because you're two feet taller than me, doesn't mean I won't kick your ass." She looks at me. "I'm Morgan Penddragon, Alex's sister."

I shake her hand. "Gwen."

"Well, you are welcome to stay here for as long as you

can. I'll kill anyone who dares touch you." She leans in and whispers, "including him."

She winks while gesturing with her elbow towards her brother.

"Why?" I ask. She looks at Alex with a raised brow and he shrugs. "Is there something going on I don't know about?"

"Who's hungry?" Morgan scrambles off to the kitchen and I catch Alex's arm before he can walk away too.

"You said you'd keep nothing from me again." I look at him and he swipes a hand down his face.

"How about tonight? I need to have a conversation with my sister first. It concerns safety and magic, nothing you'd understand." I let go of him and cross my arms as dread fills me.

"Oh, so because it's a shifter thing, you don't trust the human." I scoff and walk away from him until I find the hallway bathroom and close myself inside before turning on the tap to splash water on my face.

Pulling out my phone, I dial Tori.

"Gwen? You okay?" The grogginess is gone, but the concern is still potent.

"Yeah, what about you and Diliha?"

"I'm here, too." They're still together? That is new.

"Are you having a permanent sleep over like we all joked about when we were children?"

"No." They answer, panic lacing their voice.

"What's going on?" When they do not answer, my heart launches into a gallop.

"Nothing, we are just sticking closer together with all the stuff going on. Never mind all the boring stuff, what's up with you and shifter boy?" I smile at Tori calling him the same thing I do.

"We're in hiding."

"That's obvious. What I want to know is the juicy deets." Tori states and I wonder if I should tell them.

"Come on Gwen, we're your best friends. We would never judge you if you've been with a shifter?" Diliha's soft voice reassures me.

"We kissed." I hear them squeal and I chuckle.

"How big is he? I mean, is it true what they say about them?" Tori asks.

"What do they say about them?" I smirk.

"You know, the bigger the feet, the bigger the meat, and I mean dragons have the biggest feet I've ever seen. You know, based on the pictures." I bite my lip before answering.

"Let's just say I can neither confirm nor deny that analysis." I blush and they squeal with laughter.

"Are you happy?" Diliha asks. I ponder that for a moment.

"I don't know. I mean, he isn't what I expected, but nothing could ever truly come of this fling." I say with a somber tone.

"Nonsense, why not?" Diliha demands.

"He's a shifter. I'm a human, not to mention we come from rival courts."

"What do you mean? You're not saying what I think you are?" Tori asks, her tone grave.

"Yeah, Alex is King Outher's son." I sigh and wait for their response.

"Who fucking cares? You should get to be with whomever you want." Tori exclaims. "So, what if he isn't human? If he cares for you and treats you with respect, on top of making you happy, then why not be together?"

"It's forbidden. I could never have a shifter as my king. The people and other Courts would never accept him."

"Screw them. Valerian and Arian Court have your back."

"Thanks, but I don't think the other two will. I think we will have an all-out war."

"We are about to have one anyway."

"The armies?" I ask.

"They are assembled along the wall. Lord Pervert has reappeared at Sagittarian Court along with Prince Mauris. They are claiming you are abdicating to run off with your shifter lover." She states, and my blood boils.

"There is no way I am letting those two cowards take my throne and send my people to their deaths." I clench my fists so hard I hear a small crack in my ear. Looking at the phone, I see a crack in the screen. "What the fuck?"

"What? What happened? You okay?" Diliha asks, her voice pitching.

"Yeah, got to go. I'll talk to you later." I hang up, place the phone down and splash my face again. It cracked on its own, didn't it? There is no way…that I? No.

ALEX

I sit at the bar, sipping on the whiskey Morgan got me while I watched Gwen lock herself in the bathroom.

Morgan eyes me over the rim of her glass with a raised brow. I mimic the move, knowing what she wants to talk about, but I do not want to discuss anything with Gwen a room over.

"I like her." She says, setting her glass down. This is also after I told her that Gwen saved my life at the Inn. "She has spunk and courage."

"I know."

"Not to mention she saved your pathetic ass."

"I know." I growl at the insult.

"Then why don't you tell her?" I look away, eyeing the door, then back at my sister. "Let's step outside." She points to the balcony, and I nod, knowing I need to talk to someone other than my dragon. The doors close and we sit down on the chairs.

"My dragon claimed her." I admit.

"Figured. You have never let a human walk around killing shifters. Even if it was rightfully deserved." Morgan sips at her drink as we watch the clouds pass by.

"So, you heard about Warren?"

"Of course, I did. Every shifter in the world has heard of his death by now, including father." She sighs. "You should've ensured there were no witnesses before you left."

"I know."

"I mean, what's wrong with you? You are never this sloppy when you kill. But that is the least of your worries." I look over at her and she gulps the rest of her whiskey before elaborating further. "While you had your little rendezvous with her highness, I went to see our cousins, just like you asked me to. And the shit show they have going on is over pussy, too."

"What?" I sit up as she chuckles while shaking her head before pulling out a cigarette and lighting it.

She takes a long drag before huffing out a breath, "Princess Gwen isn't the only royal tail out there worth chasing. Rumor has it, Princess Victoria and Princess Diliha are hiding too."

"Why?"

She takes another drag of her cigarette. "Our father wants them too. Not dead, but he wants them." That motherfucker. What would he want with all three princesses? Nothing good. Why would our cousins be killing each other over this? I figured they would team up.

"And Lawrence and Junior, are they in a war over this? How does that make sense? Shouldn't they work together?"

She dabs the end of her butt out in the ashtray and leans closer to me. "They want them for themselves."

"You mean?"

"Yep. Whores, slaves, only gods know. But, in their peanut sized brains, they are staking claim to both and not sharing. They sent three assassins the night of the ball. One of them is dead, and two of them are out on the hunt." She can't mean... "Rumor has it, it was a shifter who killed the third one. Throat was ripped out and everything. And he was seen leaving with your princess."

"Fuck." I clench my fists so hard, I nearly cut through the skin of my palm. Running a hand through my hair, I let out a frustrated sigh before taking a gulp of my whiskey.

"Don't worry about our idiot cousins. They will work their

shit out. You have bigger enemies than them."

"What of the other courts? Are they in on this kidnap-murder scheme? I know Prince Mauris and Regent Warren were, but what of Prince Lance and the two princesses?" I need to be sure. I know Victoria and Diliha are Gwen's best friends, but at this point, they are guilty until I say otherwise.

"I want to say no, but I honestly don't know. Until we can find the two princesses and get a meeting with the other prince, then I cannot be sure." I think about how to handle this situation and think about confronting the Scorpion Court prince.

"Where are Prince Mauris and Warren now?"

"I was informed they are taking up residence at the Sagittarian Court, saying Princess Gwen has plans to abdicate and run-off with her shifter lover."

"That's bullshit." I jump to my feet, throwing my glass at the stone wall as my rage overcomes me. "They can't just take her throne. I will kill them. I'll kill them all for hurting her." I meet Morgan's eyes with a fierce glare. "Anyone who dares to bring pain to her will die by my hand. Anyone who so much as breathes ill-will against her, betrays, or even lies to her, will have their hearts ripped from their chest."

"Does that include you?" She cocks a brow, not showing an ounce of fear. But she has never had a reason to fear me.

"Yes. Only after I know she is safe, will I rip my heart out because gods know, I don't want to tell her." I take my seat again before she speaks.

"Why?" I sigh, knowing she is going to fight me tooth and nail on this.

"Think about it, Morgan. She is a human. I'm a shifter."

"I still don't see the issue." Morgan sighs.

I lean forward, wiping a hand down my face before pinching

the bridge of my nose, "It's forbidden. I do not even see how it's possible for her to be my mate. She's a fucking human, for god's sake." Morgan sucks her teeth.

"You're a coward, Aelxxander Penddragon." She sets her glass down before glaring at me. "Do you know how long it's been since a shifter claimed a mate?" I do, and that's part of the problem. "Don't make the mistake of letting her go before you get the chance to experience the truest form of magic."

"Having a mate isn't magical, Morgan. If it were, mother would still be alive." Meaning the mating bond magic. Mates can heal one another, even feed off their essence, but they could never bring anyone back from death.

"I'm not talking about that kind of magic, idiot."

"What else is there?" She shakes her head and sighs.

"Tell her before you don't have time to. You are now fugitives of all courts. And her life is in even more danger if she's your mate than it ever was before now." Morgan leaves me to sit and think while I sip on my whiskey, welcoming the burn. I know why she says that, because I now have a weakness that can be used against me. Only Morgan and I know the truth, and for now, that is how it will stay.

The sliding of the glass door snaps my gaze to the brown-haired beauty taking a seat in the vacant chair across from me. I look away when she does not meet my eye and wait for her to speak. After a few moments of silence, she sighs. "I broke my phone."

I turn just as she sets the cracked device on the glass tabletop. "That's fine. I can get you a new one."

"No, it's not." I look at her and see concern behind the lenses of her glasses.

"What happened?"

"I called Tori, and Diliha was still with her. Which is weird, but I guess not since I went missing." She bites her lip, my cock stirs at the sight. Now is not the time. "They know about us."

"Us?" Is she putting a label on our relationship? Does she somehow feel the mating bond? Impossible.

"Well, there is an article with a horrible picture of us. You in your shifter form, pinning me to the wall. Only, it looks like you are going to kiss me, not that I was holding my dagger against you and threatening to kill you." She sighs before tucking a loose strand behind her ear. "I told them we kissed and some other things."

"You told your best friends that we were intimate together?" I could not fight the smile spreading across my face. I laugh when I see the blush rising in her cheeks.

"Shut up. I did not say that… exactly. Only insinuated that things happened between us. Besides, that is not the point. We are in trouble. The entire world saw that picture and I am sure there are about a thousand accusations running wild. One being that I am abdicating and running off with you." She feigns a laugh. "Isn't that the most ridiculous thing you've ever heard? A princess and a shifter?"

Everything I was feeling in that moment washed away with the cold bucket of ice her words dumped over me. I was a fool to think she would want anything real. The fates have cursed me with a mate that would no sooner reject me than accept me. "Yeah. Why would I ever run away with a stuck-up human princess? When I have all the dragon tail, I could ever want."

"Yeah, so I guess that means we agree about this?" She gestures between us.

"Strictly professional from here on out." I state, leaning

forward and putting my elbows on my knees. She mimics my move, and I do my hardest to not look down her shirt.

"Good. Then what's our next move?" She looks out at the darkening skyline. Rain will come soon.

"Hide out here until I can secure a meeting with Prince Lance." She looks back at me with questions brewing in her blue eyes. "He is the only monarch that we know of who hasn't made a threat against your life."

"Tori and Diliha have not."

I wonder if I should mention the threat to her friends. If I do, she may do the irrational thing and try to warn them. That would only make them panic, and I cannot have that. I don't trust them, don't know them well enough to agree to letting her run-off and play hero. "As far as we know."

"They would never." She gets to her feet, and I do the same. "Tori and Diliha are the most loyal friends I have."

"Correction, the only friends you have, and they aren't in on all this. Which makes me decide that you no longer have phone privileges except to talk to me." She steps towards me and points an angry finger at me while snarling.

"You dick. Who do you think you are? Accusing my friends and taking my phone? Gods, if you weren't the only person I could trust, I would've gotten rid of you long before now." I step closer to her.

"You got that right, princess. I am the only one you can trust. So why don't you stop acting like a spoiled brat and listen to me for once?" She moves closer, her nostrils flaring in time with the thunder and lightning strikes. The wind picks up and blows the spray onto us, but neither of us care or moves.

"I hate you, Alex Penddragon." Her words say one thing, but the sound of her heart says another. "It would take an army to prevent me from talking to my friends, so in case you have one of those stashed away, then I suggest you get off your high horse and fuck off."

"You hate me?" I challenge. She crosses her arms and looks at the pouring rain. I grip her chin and force her to look at me. "Tell me something. If you hate me so much, why does your heart rate pick up when you see me? Your skin heats with my touch? And your tight cunt throbs when I kiss you?"

I press my lips to hers, but she bites down on my bottom lip, drawing blood before slapping me across the face. I look deep into her eyes as the rain pours down on us, soaking our clothes, outlining the perfect curves of her body. I notice the hardened peeks of her nipples poking through, and I lose all restraint.

Gripping her throat, I crush my lips to hers in a claiming kiss, penetrating her mouth with my tongue. This time she kisses me with just as much aggression, tearing at my clothes until I am shirtless. Picking her up by her ass, I do not stop kissing her as we make our way into the apartment, passing Morgan's room until reaching the guest room.

The door slams closed as I rip her jacket and shirt from her, as she tosses her glasses to the floor, somewhere. Clamping down on her hardened nipple through the lace of her bra, I reach up with one hand to unclasp it. She lets it fall to the carpet and I stake claim to both of her bountiful breasts, sucking them until they are marked by my lips.

Her fingers scratch through my wet hair before she runs the tips over my horns, eliciting a groan from me. I kiss her again as I set her feet down on the carpet.

"Are you sure?" She asks, "Because we don't have to."

I walk up to her, kneeling as I undo her pants and pull them off her body. Next, I pull her lace panties off. As she steps out of them, I look at her.

"I've wanted no one in my entire life like I want you, princess." I do not wait to hear her respond as I run my tongue through her slick folds, savoring the sweet flavor of her pussy.

CHAPTER 8

GWEN

IF I CAN ATTEST to one thing, it is that shifters know how to eat pussy, or at least Alex does.

"So fucking perfect." He groans while running his tongue through my folds again and placing a thumb on my clit. I grip his horns while I shamelessly ride his face. He adds the perfect amount of pressure, and just when I am about to go over the edge, he stops. "You didn't think I would let you cum without punishing you first, did you?"

"Fuck you." I growl as he gets to his feet.

"I plan to." He smirks before pulling me into another earth-shattering kiss. Alex does not just kiss. No, he claims. Marks his territory and makes me forget about everything else going on in this fucked up world of ours. Who cares if I let myself fall into bed with my mortal enemy? I do not, because the way he makes me feel, makes me forget, has me saying yes, every fucking time.

"Bend over, princess, and I promise to let you cum if you take your punishment like a good girl." I shudder with anticipation as I make my way over to the bed. Getting on all fours at the edge, I bit my lip as I waited for his hand to smack my ass. I am not ashamed to say it turns me on, knowing what I will get in the end. "Five, for each time you raised your voice to me."

They never hurt, like you think they might. The burn simply intensifies each time his hand smacks down, sending waves of pleasure down to my dripping core. "Harder." I moan and he chuckles before he intensifies the power, and my knees jolt slightly as I feel myself getting close to the edge. One more bit of pain, and I will have my release. "Give it to me, harder."

I hear him hum before two fingers thrust inside me, causing me to clench down and moan. "You're soaking, princess. If I had to guess, you're about ready to burst. You like the pain; it's getting you off."

"Are you going to finish your punishment, or finger fuck me?" I growl, baiting him. He pumps his fingers inside me and then smacks my ass so hard, I jolt forward and climax at the same time. My pussy milks his fingers as his other hand rubs the spot on my ass.

"So, fucking perfect." He pulls those fingers out of me and crawls behind me. One arm wraps around my waist, pulling me against his chest. "Taste yourself." I look at him while I suck my own juices from his fingers. "That's one. I plan to give you four more before the day and night is over."

I spit his fingers out of my mouth, remembering what happened to him. What his father forced him to do. "We don't have to go any further, you know, if you don't want to."

"Do you feel this?" He runs his hard cock along my folds, making me moan with the unfamiliar sensation. "I want you."

"Although I am a human?" I ask, anticipating the rejection.

"Yes." He stops at my entrance before he pushes in. We both moan at the contact. "Do you want me, although I am a shifter?" I sink down on him, stretching until he is completely sheathed inside me.

"Yes." I moan and look at him over my shoulder. He captures my lips as he moves inside me.

"Grip the headboard and hold on, because I am going to fuck you so hard. Everyone will know this pussy belongs to me." I reach out for the headboard, only falling short with a laugh. He grips my hips and moves us as one unit until I have a tight grip on it.

"Fuck me hard and fast." I tell him, and he groans as he pounds into me from behind. The girth of him has my walls stretching like they never have before. The feeling of him inside me has something within my mind awakening. A feeling, just like before calling to me. I hold on and my world blurs.

Voices, so many voices are speaking incoherently to me all at once and then nothing. My eyes flutter open and Alex is calling my name. "Princess, fuck, Gwen, talk to me."

"What, what happened?" I ask sitting up. I notice he has boxers and a black t-shirt on, and I look down and see I am wearing a white lace nightgown. "And why am I dressed?"

"You don't remember?" He looks confused.

"The last thing I remember is you fucking me. Then nothing." His cheeks go red, and I realize this is the first time I have seen him blush. "Oh gods, did I pass out before we finished?"

"Well," he runs a hand through his hair, "before I did."

"Explain."

"I don't know if it's the shifter-human thing, but you screamed my name, came all over my dick, and passed out at the same time. When I saw you were unconscious, I pulled out. I was worried I killed you." A bubble of laughter forms in my throat as I look at him.

"Oh, my fucking gods." I laugh so hard tears fall. "You fucked my pussy into a coma." I continue laughing, and Alex gives me a confused look again. "Lighten up, shifter boy. That's a compliment."

"Is it? Because to me, none of this shit is funny." He gets off the bed and storms out of the room, killing my laughter with the mood. *Way to go, Gwen, you just pissed him off again. He will punish me for another orgasm. Oh, gods, stop being selfish and talk to him.*

Getting off the bed, I make my way to the door and open it. I look around and see all the lights are off except the patio. When I expect to see him, I only see bright pink pixie hair and smoke coming from a cigarette. I grab the throw blanket off the bed, wrapping it around my body before making my way to the patio. I open the door and step out. This might be stupid, considering I do not know her, but Alex trusts her, so I can too, right?

"He isn't here." She says without looking at me.

"Yeah, I figured as much. Since it's my fault he left."

She shrugs her shoulders before taking a long drag of nicotine. I take the empty seat Alex sat in before our fight and look at the stars shining above us. "Do you believe in fate?" Her question surprises me. I do not answer it fast enough. "Because I do. Hell, all shifters do."

"Some humans do." I sigh.

"Yeah, but not you." She states more than asks.

"I believe that our actions have consequences and fate shouldn't be used as a scapegoat." She chuckles and I smile as the awkwardness subsides. "What is fate to a shifter?"

"That is a good question, with many answers. The main one is fated mates." She does not look at me while she stubs her cigarette out. "Our parents were the last of our kind. I have not seen a mating ritual since I was a child. It is the most precious thing to us shifters. Finding our mate. There can only be one."

"Does Alex have one?" The question slips before I can stop it.

"That's for him to say. My brother had a tough life after our mother was killed by humans."

"He told me what your father did to him. Forced those women to do to him."

She sighs. "That's not even the worst of it."

"What do you mean?" She does not answer me and my heart thunders in my chest.

"When he talked about his eighteenth birthday present, did he tell you everything?" I nodded, assuming.

"He was tied down, and they forced him."

"Yes, but did he tell you he was gagged the entire time? Unable to speak or be heard. His dragon was locked down because the day our mother died is the day Alex let go of everything he ever cared about, including shifting." I cup my mouth. "I don't know if I should tell you the entire story, but I will tell you, you are the first and only woman that man has ever kissed in his entire life."

"Oh, come on, now you're lying." She shook her head. "You mean to tell me, in his entire thirty years, he's kissed no one before me?"

"Never had the desire to." I flinch at the sound of his voice. "I got it from here, Sis."

"Goodnight, Gwen." She walks inside and closes the door, leaving me and him alone again.

"Why didn't you tell me?" I turn around to face him.

He shrugs. "It didn't seem important."

"Why? Because I am a human?" I ask, meeting his eyes.

"Yes," he pauses, "and no."

"Which is it? Yes or no?" He lets out a frustrated breath that has me teetering on the edge of fury and tears.

"It's complicated. I do not want to talk about it. Can we just go inside and fall asleep in each other's arms again?" He reaches out for me. I step away.

"No. It's time you are honest with me about everything. Is this a game for you?" I stare him down and create as much space as I can between us.

"No, but there are just some things better left unsaid."

"Better for who?" I demand. When he does not answer me, I know then that despite him saving my life, I cannot truly trust him. Turning away from him, I go to Morgan's door so I can get some new clothes.

"What's up?" She asks through a haze of sleep.

"I need some clothes." She looks behind me and then back at me before leading me into her room. I close and lock her bedroom door, praying to the gods that I am not about to make the biggest mistake of my life. Correction, second, because the biggest is letting myself feel something for a shifter.

"Have your pick." She motions to the dresser, and I pick out a red top and black pants with socks. "I have brand new, unused bras and panties in the top drawers." I open it and grab an ivory sports bra and comfortable cotton underwear. Moving to the bathroom, I close the door and quickly dress. I will have to grab my boots before I leave.

I turn the shower on, praying she will fall back asleep before I come out. After the shower, I turn it off and creep towards the door. Opening it, I peek out and walk towards the bed, seeing that she is asleep.

I unlock the bedroom door, creep out, and look around, seeing Alex fast asleep on the couch. I pause, my chest tightens as I look at him, he figured he was not welcome in my bed, I inhale steadily, steeling my spine as I roll my eyes and stick my middle finger at him. I make my way to the bedroom, pull on my boots and glasses before throwing on the leather jacket I never want to part with.

I think about leaving a note, but then tell myself it is not worth it. Goodbye, Shifter boy.

I step onto the deck of the ship that I paid my way by a simple hand of duces and pull the hood up further to cover my hair. I have been on my own for two weeks now, bouncing between cities, playing my hand at cards until I finally possessed enough coin to take me to my destination across the Black Sea.

With no phone to contact Tori or Diliha, I decided it was best to stay away from them. Not because some bright eye shifter planted a seed of doubt in me, but because that is where he would expect me to go. I can hear him say it now, 'knew I'd find you here, princess.' Then he would threaten me with a punishment that would have my pussy throbbing, and I cannot have that.

That is why I am walking underneath the black banners of the X-Nax Crew, privateers, and tradespeople from what I recall learning about them at court. They deliver cargo to and from each port connected to the Black Sea, Walloon City, Lirian Court, and Scorpion Court. My days at court seem like a lifetime ago compared to the past two and a half weeks.

I walk over to the right-side railing and look out at the vast sea. From my point of view, it looks like a sheet of glass, only I cannot see what lies beneath it. There are stories of sea monsters and carnivorous beasts, but I stopped believing in bedtime stories a long time ago. The actual monsters are the ones who look like ordinary people, using the human face as a mask to hide their darkest secrets.

"Weigh anchor!" The sound of one of the crew members snaps me out of my daze. Looking around, two of them haul up the plank, while ten others pull the lines back onto the deck before the sail drops, and the wind kicks the ship into gear. With all the technological advances of our time, I figured there would be magic or an invention to make this go faster. But as all the elders of this world say, 'if the gods deem it, then so be it.'

Looking down at the cracked face on the watch I swapped

off some unsuspecting bystander, I see it is quarter past noon, which means it will be this time when we arrive in Scorpion Court's Port City, Toad City, Known for their rich mercury and sulfur goods. Used for medicinal, or so I was told growing up.

"All passengers below deck." I look over my shoulder, spotting a man with deep brown skin, black hair, and honey-colored eyes, directing everyone through the wide hole in the center of the deck. I make my way over to it, ensuring I keep my face covered from prying eyes. Ever since leaving Morgan's apartment, I wear a cloth over the bottom half of my face to hide my identity, because anyone with access to a phone or computer, hell even printed articles, would have seen mine and Alex's photo by now.

"Do I know you?" I do not glance up at the question, pretending it was not directed at me while I take the first step down the ladder leading to the lower level. Putting my next foot down, I let myself believe I am in the 'all-clear,' but I clearly am not when my shoulder is jerked back with the force of a hurricane, making me knock into the crowd behind me.

"What the hell?" I get to my feet, unsheathing my new daggers at the same time. Scanning the five faces, I look for the one that just assaulted me, but cannot figure out who it is. My options are two pirates and a small family of three clinging to each other. That narrows it down to the two very tall, very muscular male pirates with doubled edged swords compared to my daggers.

"Put them down your highness, it's clear we have the upper hand." The one on the right, I will name him buck tooth because of his giant front teeth sticking out of his mouth over his bottom lip. A gust of wind blows the cloth from my face.

"I've had worse odds." I spit back with a smile on my face.

A smile that hides the fact that my heart is thundering in my chest.

"We don't want any trouble." The black-haired one speaks while shielding the three passengers. I look between the five of them. The family cower together, the child whimpering as the mother stares at me like I'm a walking nightmare. Are they scared of me?

"We won't, as long as you leave me alone while I take my ride across the sea. Once I step off this ship, you'll never see me again." I have never negotiated with pirates before; I don't even think I am supposed to unless it is the captain or something like that.

"Get down the stairs and close the hatch. I'll deal with this one." A different, feminine voice comes from behind me and I turn quick enough to connect my daggers with her sword.

"But Captain?" One of the man's protests and, without breaking eye contact with me, she lets out a low growl in warning. They scramble away until I hear the hatch close. Then it's just me and her.

"Captain?"

Her love for the color of pink matches my own, as her blouse and hair color match that of many of my clothes back home. The warm chocolate color of her eye's swirls with curiosity, not hate nor fear as she eyes me from head to toe.

"Aye, and you're our lovely princess, I suspect." She states, while cocking her head sideways.

"In the flesh."

"As much as I would love to get to know ye, I don't really like traitors on my ship wandering around for free."

"Traitor? Is that what they are calling me now?"

"Amongst other nasty words. Would you like me to tell

you?" I can hear the sarcasm in her voice and see it written all over her fair-skinned face. Not a speck of dirt or a scar to be seen.

"If you weren't threatening me right now, I'd like to think we could be friends but, since you have me at your blade's edge, I suppose we cannot." I knock her blade away from me, catching her off guard as I back away, creating more space between us. She is right in front of me in the blink of an eye, too fast for any human. She swings her sword at me. I block it with my daggers, and push away from her. "Shifter?"

"No." She answers with a smile as we continue our dance of strikes and blocks. I knock her sword from her hand, placing my blades at her throat at the same time her knee meets my gut, making me double over in pain. "You're pathetic." The taste of copper fills my mouth as her knee meets my jaw. I spit my blood onto the deck, trying to get a hold of surroundings again.

My daggers fall from my hands as she grips my hair, wrenching it backwards to make me look at her.

"What a pathetic excuse for a princess. I imagine that's why even the infamous Mafia King kicked you to the curb." She hums while running a finger along my jaw, gripping my already sore chin before digging her nails into my skin. "You spread your royal legs for him and once he realized what an easy, naïve, stupid little girl you are, he threw you out like yesterday's trash, because that's exactly what you are."

"You think your words can hurt me?" I chuckle and her face turns into a scowl as she releases my chin before her knuckles come across my face, making blood drip down my nose and mouth. My glasses are somewhere on the deck, cracked, or smashed, no doubt. She pulls a dagger from her within her vest and angles it over my heart.

"No, but I can kill you and accept the reward for bringing your head to King Outher." Somehow, inside my deep, demented, broken soul, a laugh burst through. Not just a half-hearted one, no, one that had blood spurting from my mouth onto her. "Shut up, whore, because once I am done with your head, I will cut your heart out, deliver it to your traitorous lover, then kill him next."

My laughter instantly dies as she makes her last threat. "What did you just say?" A menacing smirk forms on her face, while she leans forward to whisper in my ear.

"I'm going to deliver your heart to Alexxander Penddragon before I kill him, too." Something inside me snaps, causing my vision to blur red, like before at the Inn, when his life was in danger. I saw red as something awoke inside of me. Latching onto it, I grip her throat and squeeze, lifting her into the air as I get to my feet. "Stop." She chokes out, slashing at my arm, but I do not feel it. I am numb to everything except the rage that her threat brought on.

"You threatened him and now you die." With a firm grip on her throat, I throw her against the back post. The sound of her bones crunching on impact sings in my ears. Walking up the ten wooden steps to get to her, she gasps for air, holding up a single hand.

"Please. I... I can help you." She begs. The Gwen that existed before I was attacked, kidnapped, threatened, and assaulted, would have been lenient, merciful, but she is dormant. Now there is a beast rising from the depths of my soul, shrouding the light in darkness, and she is thirsty for blood.

"Gwen." I halt mid-step at the sound of a familiar voice. Turning my head, all the red dissipates as my eyes catch onto the last person I expected to be aboard this ship.

CHAPTER 9

ALEX

The morning after Gwen left

SIPPING ON MY COFFEE, I look out over the balcony, watching a flock of birds fly north for the upcoming cold season. Imagine if all species migrated to a different cardinal direction every time the temperature changes, there would be chaos.

The sliding door opens, and Morgan strides in. "Where's your princess? Still getting her beauty rest?"

"Gone." One word and I give Morgan a minute to realize what I said before looking at her. Just as I predicted, her eyes are wide before they narrow into a scowl.

"You stupid idiot! You let her walk out of here?" She shakes her head, but I have had it with her name calling.

"I didn't make her. She left on her own accord."

"But you could've stopped her."

"I was sleeping." That was a lie. I heard her leave and my heart crumpled at the sound of the front door closing.

"Gods!" Morgan throws up her hands before pulling out a smoke and lighting it. "I can't believe you let your mate walk away. Knowing how much danger awaits her."

"She can protect herself."

I watch as she puffs out smoke, preparing myself to take the ass chewing I rightfully deserve.

"It doesn't matter. She is your mate. Everything about us is about protecting and treasuring what is ours. What happened? Before she came and asked me for clothes, I thought you were doing your thing in the bedroom." I swipe a hand down my face, not sure if I want to tell her.

"We started to, but something happened when she, you know, and she blacked out." This is so stupid, not to mention humiliating. Especially with the bubble of laughter about to leave her mouth. "Don't laugh. It isn't funny."

"Oh, come on, it's a little funny." She pinches her thumb and forefinger together, making me laugh. "Look, if you're going to fill me in on your first-time having sex with a woman, then I need to hear everything. Okay? I'm not here to judge you. I'm here to help you." When she said 'first time I had sex', it made me realize I willingly let myself go there with Gwen. Despite my past trauma.

"Fuck. I'm an idiot." I drag a hand down my face, rubbing the hair along my chin.

"Yeah, but let us decide if you're a redeemable one at the end of this story. After she passed out, I assume you put a stop to everything?"

"Yes. And I told her what happened when she woke up. She laughed, and I was humiliated. That is why I left the first time.

When she came out onto the deck, she wanted to know more about me, and I just didn't want to talk about it." She crosses her arms and looks at me, waiting for me to continue. "That's it."

"You sure? Was anything about her being a human and you a shifter brought up at all? Because that seems to be the only thing stopping you two from crossing over into the bridge of a forbidden love story."

"There might have been something." I murmur, Morgan scoffs, "But I don't understand why it made her leave?"

"Look, Gwen has feelings for you and you not telling her, shows her you do not truly trust her. So, in the mind of anyone with a brain, that means she doesn't trust you. She is running before you have the chance to break her heart."

"I'd never hurt her."

"I know that, but she doesn't. Actions speak louder than words, brother."

"You think I should go after her?"

"Better. We both should. I would like to get to know my future queen and best friend." I cock a brow at her. "She is your mate. I am your general and sister. It's bound to happen."

"Have you seen her or not?"

It has been four days and still no sign of her. I have scoured Rose City looking for any witnesses to her last known location and I have come up empty-handed. Now I am desperate, especially if I have made my way into the confines of Sagittarian's forgotten city, Tempress.

Buildings with dry-rotted walls and ceilings, streets that smell of piss and shit; it is no wonder the court stopped caring for it. At this moment, I am in what could be considered the 'lavish' side of town. Even run-down cities need a mayor to govern it. That is who I am speaking with now. Mayor Koshi. Criminal mastermind and drug dealer of Sagittarian Court. I have had no qualms with him, as long as dealings did not involve the innocent.

"Why is the princess of any interest to a Mafia Don? Especially a human one at that." Koshi asks while twirling one of his many emerald rings around his finger. Green is the color of vomit, and this man is obsessed with it. Green hair, suit, and eyes. I will say they complement the darker complexion of his skin.

"Haven't you heard? My father has placed a bounty on her. He wants her brought in alive and unharmed." A twisted lie but it was my luck that Koshi does not deal with technology or else he would have heard the rumor mill spinning our little love story.

"You know as well as I do, I trade in goods, not people." He puffs out smoke from his cigar before placing it down on the emerald ash tray. "But I have eyes everywhere in this court. I can have my people report any sighting directly to me." I know as well as the next man, information does not come for free. That is why I wait for the catch. "For the right price, of course."

"Of course. How much?"

"Free rein of my product in all your territories."

"Not going to happen." I clench the arms of my chair,

baring my teeth at him.

"Then I'm afraid we've reached an impasse." He folds his hands over his rounded belly, giving me a smug smirk. "Tell me something, is this princess worth turning down a resource such as me?"

"The only thing you are resourceful for is a nice high. I imagined if you spent as much time and effort in this city as you do in your illegal drug business, your pathetic little scrap of space would mean something. The princess is not worth my morals." Getting to my feet, I straighten the sleeves of my jacket before turning to leave. "Thank you for your time."

I make it halfway to the door before he speaks. "Fine. If you split the profit of turning her over with me, I will ensure none of my product so much as tip toes into your territory."

"Pleasure doing business with you." I turn the knob and leave. Knowing the bogus deal will make my list of enemies longer, but if it means finding her again, then so be it. I will deal with the aftermath later.

"Are you sure you can trust him?" Morgan asks as the door closes behind me and we walk down the narrow hall that leads to the outside of the building. She was not keen on the idea of going to this gods' forsaken city.

"No, but what other choice do I have? The man has more connections than I do. Especially now that I am on every assassin's list within a ten-mile radius." It was two days into our search when I got the call from my father.

"What in god's name are you thinking?" He growls on the other end of the line.

"At this moment, I'm thinking of hanging up on you."

"You worthless little wretch. If you think I will let you get away with this, this betrayal-"

"I don't think, I know you will, because you haven't heard of my plan yet." The line goes silent.

"It better be a good one. Or your little princess will not be the only head being delivered to me." I stop myself from growling at him for threatening her, and instead reveal my diabolical plan, to him.

"The princess is just out of reach, but I can play double-agent. Make her believe I am on her side, then once she fully trusts me, I will hand deliver her head to your doorstep." My heart thunders in my chest as I wait for him to call my bluff. My father is a ruthless, cold-hearted bastard, but he is not a fool.

"You have three days. If I do not have her head as you have promised, your name goes on the hit list. Don't think this means I trust you, because we both know you destroyed any hope of that the day you killed your mother." He hangs up on me, delivering his last stab at my heart.

Four days later and I have yet to deliver Gwen's head. I have not had contact with my father since, but we know he has out-casted me by the attempt on my life yesterday as we stepped out of Morgan's apartment for the first time since Gwen left.

"Alex, what about her friends? Diliha and Victoria, would she go to them?" Morgan asks, pulling me out of my head. We walk down a dark alley, heading the direction of the Farce and Tempress City border. That is our next destination.

"No, she wouldn't go to them. Gwen knows that if she does, her friends' lives will be at risk." I answer as I look up at the sky and think of her. I am not one for prayer, but if the gods can hear me, I pray for my princess because she is not just my mate, she is my heart.

"Do you think she took a ship out of here?" Morgan asks as

we walk across the bridge leading into the next city on my list. We could fly, it would be faster, but also announce our arrival everywhere we land. Morgan is putting herself in danger of being seen with me, and if anything happened to her, I'd never forgive myself.

"No. I know she hasn't left the continent. I can still feel her presence. She is close by, but it seems as if every time we get closer to her, she vanishes for a while. I don't know how that's possible." They say the mating bond has a sensation between two souls. They always know where the other is. Only Gwen and I do not have that connection. I know she is my mate because of my dragon, but she does not.

That could be the reason this tether I feel for her is weakened by the distance between us. It is false hope that it will happen. There has never been a human shifter relationship; at this rate, there may never be.

"Where are we starting this time?" Morgan asks as we walk down the quiet main road of the downtown market. Something doesn't feel right about this place. Looking at my watch, I see it is way too early for the shops to be closed and the streets to be empty.

"Something's wrong."

"What?"

"It's nearly six, and no one is outside." I look around, reaching into my jacket to grip the hilt of the blade I started carrying with me, and listen. Out of the corner of my eye, I see Morgan ready herself for an attack, telling me she senses it, too.

The whooshing of a fireball just barely missing the right side of my head as the charge of an ambush rings in the air. One by one, shifters reveal themselves with the light of their own flames dancing in the palms of their hands.

"Prince Alexxander Penddragon, you're an enemy of the state and I, Joan Baleick, am going to kill you and bring your father your head." I see him now. White and red stripes lining the mohawk running down the middle of his head. A ripped jean jacket vest draped over a long-sleeved shirt, which covers his torso just above the waistband of his black pants. Chestnut brown boots cover his feet as he approaches me.

"Baleick, last I heard, you were shipped to my father's prison for petty theft. And he took your hand." I look and see him wearing one glove on his right hand, while his left wields a fireball. "And you are not a shifter, yet you stand here wielding our power."

"Courtesy of my king and rightful ruler of Constellinia." Not possible. The only beings ever able to grant powers are the gods themselves. "Don't wrap your brain around it. If it is your dying wish, I will let you know how it's possible."

"The only one dying tonight is you." Morgan growls.

"Don't worry sweet cheeks, I don't have orders to kill you. Only to deliver you to the boss man." Baleick winks at her. The biggest mistake he will ever make.

"You see, the problem with men is that they see women and think we are easily intimidated. But you know what I see when I look at you?" She questions him, giving me an opportunity to strike. Closing my eyes, I call upon my dragon before opening them again. Through his eyes, I see all five shifters surrounding me.

"What's that?" He asks her, not sparing me another glance. I do not want to kill them all, just wound them. Summoning my fire, I shoot out towards all of them, knocking them ten feet away while Morgan pins Baleick beneath her with a dagger to his throat.

"I think you should spill your last secret before you descend into hell." She growls.

"Not a chance." He tries to wriggle free, and I snarl at him.

"Tell me how you got shifter power." I growl at him, but he does not take his eyes off my sister.

"Tell him." She digs the blade in deeper.

"Kiss me." I could not stop what happened next. The sound of the blade cutting his throat open was not the worst sound I have heard. It was him drowning in his own blood that got me.

"Seriously, Sis?" She gets off him, not before wiping her blade clean on his shirt.

"You know how I feel about traitors. Besides, men like him don't squeal so easily." She sighs, getting to her feet.

"We need to get moving. The others will have awoken by now." I grab her elbow as we step around the dead body and move past the first couple of buildings. The hairs on the back of my neck raise as I sense another threat, only this time, I am not quick enough to save myself.

As the world slows, I shove her into the dark alley while the iron chains wrap around my wrists and ankles, cutting off the access to my dragon. Morgan's eyes widen as she catches onto what is happening.

Stay.

Hide.

Run.

When the iron helmet closes around my head, my entire world goes dark.

GWEN

"Morgan?" With her hands raised in a gesture of surrender, I look down at myself and something breaks when I see the blood painted on my hands.

My knees buckle and I fall to the deck as tears flow down my face. Two small hands cup my wet, swollen cheeks and lift my heavy head up with ease.

"What happened?" I look into her purple eyes. Eyes I never thought I would see again. But I do not answer her question because all I smell is him. All I want to hear is his voice, feel the caress of his hand against my skin while I soak in his fiery scent.

"Where is he?" My voice croaks and then I see it. I swallow the lump down and it goes with protest, as do my unshed tears. "He's gone, isn't he?"

"I know where he is." I shove her hands away and pick myself up. Morgan stands to her full height, just a head shorter than me.

"I will save him, but only after I deal with her." I point at the bleeding pirate captain as I pick up a fallen dagger.

"Morgan?" The captain speaks.

"Mordrid? Fucking hell, what'd you do to piss her off?" I hear Morgan ask her.

"She threatened to kill Alex after she tried to kill me." Having Morgan here to watch me throw this dead bitch to the sea only edges me on further.

"Seriously? You're back to that?" I push past Morgan, raise up my dagger, and bring it down. Only it does not meet its target. "Gwen, listen to me. Cool off. You don't want to kill her."

She has a fire shield blocking my attack.

"Yes, I really do." I snarl. "Move, Morgan, I don't want to hurt you."

"Gwen, look at me. This isn't you."

"I am, Morgan. Believe me, it's new to me too, but I can't let people go around hitting me or threatening me anymore." She presses more magic against me.

"He wouldn't want you like this. Becoming a merciless killer." I shake my doubts away.

"Why are you protecting her? I thought you were loyal to him?" A thought crosses my mind and I narrow my eyes at her. "You betrayed him, didn't you?"

"No, Gwen. There was an ambush, and I will tell you everything, but you need to back off." Red clouds my vision again. The pull inside me resurfaces and I grip onto it. "Gwen, listen to me. Calm down and we will save him, together. Please, look into my eyes and tell me if I am lying to you."

"I don't believe you." I growl and slam down hard on her shield. I feel it waver, so I repeat my attack.

"You're his mate!" She screams the words, but they do not register. "You're his fucking mate." I slam down on the shield again, feeling it shudder beneath my dagger.

Wait…

Air rushes between my teeth.

Mate?

Everything goes from red to black in the blink of an eye.

Icy water splashes against my face as I snap awake, wiping a hand down my face. "Now she's awake."

"And pissed."

"Morgan?" I blink through the fog of my eyes until I see her face.

"Welcome back, princess. Oh, here you go." She hands over my glasses, which I am surprised are still intact.

"What happened?" I ask, wiping my eyes before slipping them on my face.

"I showed up before you killed her and then you passed out." She says the last part quickly, giving me an awkward smile. I look over and see who Morgan is talking about.

"I'm waving a white flag here, princess. So please, don't go all beastly on me again." Mordred, if I remember what Morgan called her before she said…

"Alex is my mate?" I ask Morgan. Ignoring the pirate captain.

"I was hoping you didn't remember that part because once he finds out I told you, he's going to kill me."

"How long has he known?" I ask her, trying to recall every moment we spent together.

"After your first time being intimate." She sighs and I look away, because I would hardly call what we have done intimate. "If it is the whole human shifter thing freaking you out, I honestly think it's the coolest damned thing to happen in the history of things. I mean, just imagine what the gods were thinking."

"Morgan, why didn't he tell me? I mean, it happened before I left, but why?" Her smile fades and she claps my hand.

"Honey, my brother is a ruthless man, but the one thing he isn't is smart. He was a damned fool to let you walk away."

"He wasn't the only one." I sigh as I run my fingers through my hair. "Wait, did you heal me?"

"Yeah, that's something else we got to figure out. Are you sure you're fully human?" I give her an incredulous look.

"Yeah, why?" She looks towards Mordred, who nods encouragement. Which has my anxiety spiking.

"Because you have magic. Somehow, you healed yourself. And you had super strength I have never seen before. No human can do any of that." I try to think of a way to make this make sense, with me losing control over my anger. Killing shifters, breaking metal.

"But my parents were human, I'm sure of it." I watch as my two companions have some silent conversation, and it pisses me off. "What aren't you saying?"

"Should I tell her?" Mordred asks.

"Tell me what?" I look between the two of them, my eyes going frantic.

"The origins of the blood feud between our two worlds." Morgan states.

"It's because of King Outher. He wants to enslave all humans, right?" I ask.

"Yes, but that's not the origin story." Morgan says.

"Tell me." I swallow as Mordred pulls up a chair. I look around and realize we are in a cabin aboard the ship.

"Five centuries ago, Constellinia was one Kingdom. There were six courts. Shifters and humans lived in harmony. Every

summer solstice, the monarchs for each court would meet at the very center, Star Palace, and celebrate their unity. But the most notable friendship was between the shifter prince and sapphire court prince and princess. Prince Bash, Princess Alina, and Prince Killian grew up together. Only Alina and Killian had a secret they were keeping from her brother. And her betrothed"

"Killian, we have to stop this. I am engaged to be married." Alina tries to reason with Killian. In his heart, he knows she is his one and only.

"Alina, please marry me instead. We are together." Killian argues, but Alina will not break.

"My wedding is tomorrow." Killian cups her soft cheek before whispering against her lips.

"Then give me one more night to love you." He kisses her lips, waiting for her to protest.

"One more." She whispers, letting her heart take control as she deepens it. In the Fields of Sarssaraland, Killian and Alina made love for the first and last time. On the night of her wedding to Prince Edward, she gave her body to him out of duty, but her heart remained with another.

When it was time for her monthly blood, it did not come, and the affair she had with her one true love came to life nine months later in a pool of blood and water. It was the birth of Killian and Alina's son that killed her. Edward raised the baby with spite in his heart and when it came time for him and Killian to be reunited, it was on the battlefield where Killian left his heart.

"You betrayed me, Killian." Edward yells.

"You kept my son from me." Killian roars. "My only heir. And the last thing she ever gave to me."

"He wasn't supposed to be yours." Edward screams.

"Alina was mine. But because of your stupid laws, she was too afraid to leave you and marry me. But she gave herself to me, on this very field, the night before you stole her away from me." Killian snarls. "And now I have come for my son."

"No. There is no evidence beyond our knowledge that he is a half-shifter. He has no horns or wings or pointed ears. The only way I knew, is because she told me. I only wished it wasn't true, but when the test performed by the witches came back, it confirmed it." Edward states. "You killed her, Killian. You and your bastard son."

"As they fought to their death, the boy remained with his uncle in Valerian Court." She finishes.

"But how does that relate to me?" I ask.

"Isn't your mother from Valerian Court? She would have carried the line of shifter blood." Morgan asks.

"Yes, but what about Alex? I mean, he isn't a part of the line that carries Killian's blood, right?" Gods, I would hate to think we were related. No matter how distant.

"No, my father killed Killian's last living descendant before he took the throne. It was long before any of us were born." Morgan states reassuringly.

"It seems like humans aren't the only ones who have civil wars." I joke, trying to break the tension. "So, I may have shifter blood running through my veins. What should I do? Should I talk to Tori? I mean, she could too, right?"

"I don't think talking to anyone else about this is the smartest move." Morgan says. "But I suggest until we understand what is going on with you, I think you should do your best to control your emotions. Anger seems to be the source of your power."

"I think so too. But what about Alex? When was the last

time you saw him? Is he alive?" The questions pour out one after the other, and I slow down when she pinches my lips together.

"He is beyond the wall." She states as she lets my lips run free. "We will need an army to get to him."

"Where are we going to get one of those?" I ask, knowing that mine is off limits.

"Well, you booked this charter for Scorpion Court, so I suggest we start with Prince Lance." Morgan smiles and I go for a hug, because sometimes, I just really need one of those. I can sense she is shocked when she does not immediately hug me back, but then she embraces me with a tight squeeze. "We'll get him back, Gwen, on pain of death. I swear we will."

"Even if it means burning the world down in my wake, I will save him. I will save my mate." A clapping sound ruptures from next to us and we both break our hug to look at Mordred, wiping away false tears. "Are you sure I shouldn't kill her?"

"Nah, she isn't so bad once you get to know her." I catch Morgan's sidelong glance and I see it.

"You two have history, don't you?" I catch the blush rising in her cheeks before she smiles at me.

"Yeah, we do."

"Is that why you saved her?" She looks back at me, the smile fading.

"No, Gwen, I didn't save her for anyone but you."

"Me?"

"If you killed her, it would've changed you. Darkened your soul. You are not a merciless killer. You are a badass. I just couldn't picture you being the real you if you would've killed her like that." I sigh, thinking she is right, but something still has me doubting her.

"Morgan, never come between me and a kill again. I will defend myself and those I care about. Just as you do. She would not be the first person I killed to save myself or someone else. You know that." I called her on that shit because I couldn't care less, but for Morgan, I will give Mordred a chance.

"See, badass." We spend the rest of the evening discussing how to address the prince once we arrive. Should I go incognito or show up at his front gates? As they blabber, my mind drifts to him. *I am your mate and you never told me. Why didn't you tell me? Who am I? What is this darkness inside me?*

"Gwen, wake up." I hear Morgan yell at me before she tosses something at me. A pillow, I think.

"Five more minutes." I groan, burying my face between the sheets. We have been at sea for three days, including the first day Mordrid and I fought each other. During the time, we spent it strategizing the next step in the plan.

"I will give you five to get dressed and ready to go. Remember what the goal here is. Get an army, kill my father, save your mate." She reads off the synopsis of our plan, and with it, I get myself up and dressed before the fifth minute is up.

"Coffee?" Morgan hands me a steaming cup as I step out on deck dressed in an all-black pirate outfit. Or at least, that is what I would call this get up. It is my disguise to throw off my normal appearance, which, according to Morgan and Mordred, is pretty in pink.

"Yes, thank you. Are we sure this is a clever idea?" I ask them both as we stare out at the vast city. At the tallest peak is Scorpion Court's palace. Made of the crystalized gems themselves and hardened with magic, or so I have been told. I do not know what to believe about my past anymore.

"By this time tomorrow, we will meet with the prince, and hopefully leave with an army." Morgan smirks. And then I am coming for you. And anyone who stands in my way better be powerful enough to kill me, because nothing will stop me from getting what is rightfully mine.

CHAPTER 10

ALEX

DARKNESS. IT SURROUNDS ME, suffocates me as I try to search for her-my princess.

I have been in and out of consciousness since my capture. Unsure of my location, as the only holes inside this helmet are small slits for me to breathe through. They want me alive, whoever they are, or else I would surely be in the depths of hell. I have no use of my arms or legs, no access to my magic, and I feel weak for the second time in my entire life.

The heat blazing against my skin tells me I am no longer in Sagittarian Court territory, and I can rule out all the other human courts, except one, Lirian. Now the bastard prince and I have bad blood, but the scent of the air has a mixture of sulfur and ash, revealing to me the only place in all of Constellina to have a volcano.

Something raw rubs against the blisters forming on my exposed skin where my clothes are torn or missing completely.

Being dragged from one city to the next can do that to a person's clothes. My suit jacket is gone, and the soles of my dress shoes are torn. It is my fault for dressing for a business meeting rather than a person on the run.

"Easy with the merchandise, will 'ya?" A male with a southern accent state, someone from Valerian Court.

"We didn't have to deliver him alive." Another male responds.

"Aye, but she specifically requested it. And I do not know about you, but I don't want to get on her bad side." The first one states and has me thinking of what woman they are talking about. I suspected they would deliver me to my father, not a woman.

Two hands grip my forearms, hoisting me to my feet. I do not aid them, allowing myself to appear as weak as I can. Make them believe you are defeated. They will become complacent and make a mistake, then I will strike. "You'd think after two weeks, he'd be a lot lighter."

Is that how long it has been? I lost track of time, which is easy enough being trapped inside the confines of this iron helmet. My feet protest with each step. My captors practically carry me across the firm surface that shoots shards of pain up my legs. "We're here to see her."

I strain my ears, trying to hear anything that would tell me where I am and who this she is that they talk about, until I hear a click resound off the metal walls surrounding my head. The first sensation I feel is a cool mist kissing my skin as the iron is lifted. It almost seems like a dream. I am too afraid to blink my eyes until I hear her speak.

"Sorry about this, but it was the only thing I could think of to protect you." It cannot be. She would never. "Open your eyes, Alex."

My eyes burn with protest as I force myself to look at the face of my betrayer. "Why?" I croak out, my voice hoarse from not speaking for two weeks.

"As I told you that day in my office, two paths, one will lead to death and the other, well, I couldn't have that union happen. I mean a human as your mate?" Lettie grips my chin, her dark nails adding pain. "I loved your mother with all my heart."

"Don't you dare." I croak out again. My throat dries as the pain of her betrayal breaks a part of me.

"You have her eyes and her spirit." She smirks before pushing my face away. "Get him some water before he dies of dehydration." I don't spare her a glance as my eyes roam around, trying to gather my surroundings. I would recognize this place anywhere. We're back beyond the wall, inside Lettie's house.

"Our money?" One captor demands that Lettie take a seat in a chair in front of the room. Did she really turn her living room into a small throne room? Power hungry traitor. My thoughts are quiet as one of her underlings places a cup of water to my chapped lips. Slowly, I suck the water down, the warm liquid easing the tension in my throat.

"Yes, it will be transferred to you immediately." She waves them off, reluctantly, they depart and as I guzzle down another glass of water, I meet her eye.

"So, you're working with my father now?" She crosses her legs, the skirt of her violet dress shrinking to just above her knees.

"No. I'm just keeping you safe until it is all over." A coughed laugh irrupts from deep within me. I wince as the pain reverberates from my throat to my chest. "Easy, boy. With your powers suppressed, you cannot heal yourself."

"Like you care." I snarl as drool drips from my lips. "Every word you spit out of your traitorous mouth is a lie."

"No, it's not. Gwen is your mate, and you will die because of her. I swore a vow to your mother to protect you, no matter what. And if that means keeping you from her, then so be it."

"Your false sense of protection does nothing but turn every feeling of love I had for you to hate. Once I break free, and trust me, I will. You will be the first person I kill." I snarl and she gets to her feet, making her way towards me.

"As long as it means you will stay away from her long enough, then I will die by your hand." I look away from her. My stomach turns as bile rises in my throat, burning away the soothing nature of the water. "It won't matter. She'll be dead by the end of the week."

"You underestimate her."

"No, my child, it's you who underestimates me." I scoff at her ignorance.

"Gwen is a warrior and more of a woman than you will ever be. I will be damned if you think you can kill her. Hell, I'd pay to see the day she runs you through with her daggers."

"Be careful what you wish for."

"Why? Does my wish for you to die at the hands of my human mate frighten you?" I see a slight tremble in her stoic expression, and I let myself smile. "Don't worry, I'll make sure you are burned right next to my father and all traitors of the crown."

"I think you've had enough free time for today." Snapping her fingers, a door opens and two guards waltz in. "Escort him to his room. Ensure it's prepped and ready for his training." I cut my gaze back to her, and she smirks at me. "Did you think

I was going to let you rot? Oh no, by the time I am done with you, your precious Gwen won't recognize you as you deliver the final, fatal blow."

"Never." I growl.

"You are a strong shifter, Alexxander, but even shifters can't fight my magic." Her cackles echo as I am dragged from one room to the next.

My arms strain as the chains dig deeper into my wrist with each pull. I growl and fight, but it is no use once they become taut as I am locked into a brick room with my body spread out. We will fight it. I would never hurt her. Lettie will not win. Closing my eyes, I reach deep inside for my dragon. *Please, I need you now more than ever.* I know it's futile because once the iron hits the skin, all shifter magic is suppressed, making us practically human.

I never thought I would ever hear my own skin burning. The smell doesn't mask the sizzling sound the blade makes when it shreds through the top layer of my flesh.

After the first four days of being locked inside this chamber, I grew numb to the pain. With each cut and push of Lettie's dark magic through my veins, my mind escaped to a different realm. Where my only thoughts are of Gwen, my mate.

"I know what you're doing, boy." A slap to my face, a hard grip to my chin, brings me out of my head. Lettie bares her teeth at me before speaking. "You think allowing your mind to drift to your mate, will help you escape the pain. But that won't be an issue soon enough."

My arms are raised above my head by an iron chain connected to the concrete ceiling. My ankles are bound by iron clasps bolted to the floor. No clothes adorn my body besides my boxers, allowing her better access to infect me with her poison.

"You can try, but you must realize after a week, I will not falter in my loyalty to my mate. Nothing and no one will ever turn me against her." I snarl through gritted teeth.

Lettie smiles at me before cupping my cheek. "This would be a lot less painful for the both of us if you would just devote yourself to me. You would've done anything to take down the royals long before you ever laid eyes on the princess."

"That's the funny part about laying my eyes on her. My inner dragon recognized her as ours the moment I did." I smiled, letting my feelings about Gwen be exposed. She moves closer to me, allowing her overwhelming mothball scent to fill my nostrils.

"Your eyes, they match your mother's perfectly. I loved your mother with all my heart. That's why I have to protect you. I need to fix you before it's too late." She plants a kiss on my lips. I try rearing back, but my chain doesn't allow much leverage. When she finally steps away, I spit the vile taste of her from my lips.

"My mother would burn you alive for this." Lettie smiles and tilts her head to look at me.

"That's where you're wrong. Your mother was a lot of things, but disloyal to me, wasn't one of them."

"What the fuck are you lying about this time?" I growl as she turns to take a syringe filled with the same black liquid she has been infusing into my body since day one and walks back to me. Pressing the sharpened tip to the vein at the crease in my right arm.

"Hold tight. This is even stronger than the last. Soon, all you will want to do is please me." She pushes the needle in and begins pressing the liquid into my veins. The burning sensation is ten times hotter, and I wince , holding onto the scream as I struggle to break free. "Every thought you have will only be of me. When you drift away to escape the hands of your torturer, you will be with me." I close my eyes as she finishes injecting me, trying to block out her words as I clutch to the thoughts of Gwen. Slowly, every image of her is replaced with Lettie. Every sound, touch, and scent is only of Lettie, my Lettie.

I open my eyes and see her standing before me, dressed in a tight violet dress that falls just below her knees. Her gray hair is curled into a tight bun atop her head, and I lock onto her eyes. Something doesn't feel right about the way I feel when looking at her. It doesn't seem natural, but I can't figure it out.

"Alexxander, are you ready for your next training session?" She asks. I look down and see my chains are gone, and I am wearing nothing but black gym shorts. Red scars line my torso, along with small slashes against my arms. I move closer to her, the object of my newest obsession. The need isn't lustful or loving, but anger and hate. "What are you doing?"

"You should've kept me in chains, Lettie." I snarl. In the blink of an eye, I grip her throat, lifting her well above me.

"This isn't possible. My magic, I used it to turn you against her." I cock a brow, not sure who she is talking about. "Tell me you remember, I'm Lettie, your mother's best friend. Your master and you're my loyal soldier."

I hum before turning to march to the metal table I was once

strapped to. Slamming her down onto it with a loud crack, she squirms and scratches at my arm, but all the strength of my dragon has returned.

"Get off me. Obey me." She chokes out as I chain from her wrists and ankles down to the table. Once I ensure she is secured, I step back. Her eyes widen with fear as she frantically tries to free herself.

"Tell me something, Lettie, why are my only and every thought about you? I know nothing else except the memories I have between you and me. Some things are fuzzy, but I do, however, remember you strapping me down and torturing me." I cross my arms while waiting for her to answer.

"Because that's what happens when you find your mate. Every waking thought becomes only of them." I smirk at her lies.

"My mate. Lettie, when you were pushing your magic into me, you said some very conflicting things. Trying to make me forget another woman. Not sure why, if you are my mate and all." I approach her, gripping her chin hard enough to leave a bruise. "You're going to tell me the truth because whatever magic you used on me to make you my obsession, it worked. Only I hate you, not love you."

I release her chin and turn my back before I hear her cackle. Glancing over my shoulder, I see her laughing until she is bursting into tears. "That spell did backfire."

She sighs before composing herself. "Alexxander, listen to me, listen to me closely. I used my magic to help expel the threat on your life."

"The girl?" I question, turning to look at her.

"Yes. She is a human, a nasty, vile creature that wants to see you and your father's kingdom destroyed. Somehow, she got a hold of magic and used it against you. To make you believe she was your mate."

"Just like you did?" I ask, walking up to her again.

"I thought that if I could make you believe it, it would help break the spell she put on you. And look, it worked." She fearfully laughs. I close my eyes, trying to remember everything that has happened the past three weeks, but it's all blurred except the times I have been with Lettie.

"Why can't I remember what has happened the past three weeks?"

"It's the spell. Both counteracted with one another and erased some of your short-term memories. You only remember my encounters with you because I was the one fighting the other spell." A deeper part inside of me wants to doubt her words. Perhaps my dragon doesn't believe her, but I can sense no lies when my mind presents the evidence itself.

"Tell me everything from the beginning, and I might consider letting you live." I growl while I listen to her.

"Three weeks ago, before you encountered that human woman that put a spell on you, business was good. Your father was gearing up for the siege of the wall. There was a bounty put on the Sagittarian Court Princess's head and he enlisted you to kidnap her and deliver her to your father. When you left for the masquerade to intercept her, that's when she cast the spell." She sighed heavily, as if a major burden was lifted off her shoulders.

"What else? Why would my father want to siege the human courts? He can't possibly have that kind of power." I rub the hair along my chin, thinking further on it.

"Let me go and I will show you everything." She huffs out, but I won't let her sway me so easily.

"You haven't convinced me yet. Tell me how my father plans to take over the human courts. If twenty years ago, he couldn't. What's different this time?" I eye her keenly, letting her know I will not budge.

"We have a new army alongside the shifter army. Humans with shifter abilities. Some are limited, but others, they are lethal, even more so than you or I. She swallows, and for the first time, I see the heaviness in her eyes. The darkness that swims inside of her. A darkness that my inner dragon does not trust. "The day the Wall went up, the Sun Goddess morphed into a golden relic, one that has the most powerful magic I have ever seen. With it, your father started having us experiment on humans until we got the formula correct."

A pain surged in my head as a memory flashes before me where a human was wielding a fireball in his hand.

"You were successful." I grunted as the pain vanished with the memory.

"Yes, and now we have the means to take back what's rightfully ours." I run a hand through my hair, making sense of all this, but I still have more questions than answers.

"The human princess, the one who cast a spell. How did she have magic to do it?" I asked, thinking it wasn't possible. No human possesses natural power like that. "Was she working with my father?"

"No. But she must have had help from another witch shifter. One I do not know."

"Lettie, if what you're telling me is true, then that means thousands of innocent lives are about to be destroyed and I don't agree with that." I shake my head, "I may not remember the last three weeks of my life clearly, but I remember my rules and they will not falter. If you loved my mother as you claim, then you understand why I have those rules." I turn away from her, looking for more clothing but don't see any. "I need to have a word with my father before he does something stupid."

"And the princess?" I freeze in my spot at her question.

"What about her?" I turn and look at Lettie with a smile spreading across her face.

"Aren't you going to deal with her? I mean, she attacked you, manipulated you. Shouldn't that warrant a death sentence?" She asks.

"No, Lettie. I'm not my father, but I will need to speak with the princess and figure out what her motive is. Perhaps she thought that forming some type of bond with me would get my father to back off. It's understandable to take drastic measures when one's citizens are at risk." I sigh.

"And what about me?" She gestures to the chains.

"I'd like to leave you to rot, but seeing as you did what you had to, to break the spell, then I will let you go. But so, help me, Lettie, if I find out you told a single lie to me, you will be the first to die." I break the chains from her body and move to leave the room, but the door is locked.

"Can't we talk about this more? I don't think going to your father is the wisest decision right now. I mean you ran off with the princess and he thinks you betrayed him. You'll be killed the moment you step foot outside my cottage." That stops me in my tracks. Turning around, I narrow my eyes and watch as she pushes the healing magic into her joints.

"Elaborate." I growl.

"It was all over the news. You and Princess Gwen are lovers. Abdicating from your royal positions to be together. It's quite touching, really. If you like forbidden love stories and all that." She runs a hand through her hair.

"Lettie, why would my father believe this?" She looks at me with a sullen expression.

"Because when he told you to bring her to him, you refused. Now you're labeled as a traitor."

I march up to her, pointing a finger. "Why didn't you tell him what you discovered?" I glare at her, smoke emitting from my flaring nostrils.

"Because I figured the only way he would listen is once you brought her to him. As your prisoner." She smirks. "He wouldn't believe me, anyway. He blames you for your mother's death and now trusts nothing I say on your behalf." She sighs and I feel my anger be redirected toward a new person. "Alexxander, if you want to regain your father's trust, you need to capture the princess, bring her to court, and force her to confess her sins. Then and only then will you prove your loyalty to him."

I look away from her, trying to figure why I feel so conflicted by turning this princess over. What happened between me and her in the time I have lost? Why would my father be making a move against the human courts? He hates humans. Why would he grant them access to our power?

"Alex," Lettie cups my face, just like she did when I was a boy. "I can see the conflict in your eyes, but if you want to clear your name and speak with your father about this war, then you need to do this. Bring Princess Gwen of Sagittarian Court to her knees before your father. Turn her over and be rid of her, and finally gain your father's trust and respect. You owe this to your mother."

I wince at the mention of her. The only reason I lost everything was because I lured my mother across the wall, where the humans shot an arrow through her heart. If bringing down Sagittarian Court's princess is the only way to bring justice to my mother's murder and stop a war, then so be it.

"Find her and I'll do the rest." I growl and Lettie jumps in excitement. Better be prepared, your highness, because the beast is unleashed and ready to strike.

CHAPTER 11

GWEN

A S WE APPROACH THE golden gates, I pull my black
cloth mask higher, just to ensure it covers the bottom
half of my face. The worst part is my glasses keep fogging
every time I breathe. "I can't see a damn thing with this cloth
up."

"Here." Morgan reaches over, flips out a butterfly knife,
and brings it scarily close to my nose. "Hold still, Gwen." I
close my eyes and hear the cutting of fabric before I blink, and
my glasses clear up.

"Wow. Thank you." She shrugs before tucking it back inside
her jacket. We waited until dark, going with the incognito
plan to sneak in undetected and basically force the prince into
submission.

Stepping off the deck onto the dock, I scan the area for any
leftover drunks or sailors lingering nearby. Not that it wouldn't
surprise me at this dark hour. I've never been to this part

of Iticha. To say I am nervous would be an understatement. Luckily, Morgan and Mordred seem to know the layout of the land.

Following Morgan, we step off the docks onto a cobblestone path that runs down a path of multi-colored buildings. Each painted a different. "This is a rainbow row." Morgan whispers, without looking back at me.

"What is the significance of this?" I ask, curious about the different culture this land will open my eyes to.

"Rainbows symbolize peace and prosperity. Something that your court appears to be lacking. No offense." She adds, looking left and then right. We stand at the fork in the road, between the yellow and blue house. Each is a towering three stories with white framed windows and double wide doors.

"I know that my court is in discord. That is why I was looking forward to becoming Queen." I whisper back as we cross the path, melting into the shadows as our backs press against the cool brick wall of the blue house.

"I highly doubt a change in your status will bring any peace to the Sagittarian Court." She remarks. Her doubt and words cut me like a jagged edge.

"You don't believe that I could bring our home peace?" I ask her. Hating that her back is towards me. Pausing in her steps, she sighs before looking at me.

"Gwen, I'm not saying I don't believe you won't try to bring peace to our home, but the Sagittarian Court isn't the only territory that has issues." Narrowing my eyes, I look at her with suspicion in my heart.

"You know something, don't you?" She looks away, as if to hide her guilt or shame from keeping something from me. "Morgan, if there is something going on in any of the other courts, you must tell me. Especially if it is Tori or Diliha's territory."

"Look, Gwen, what's more important to you right now?" Her purple gaze intensifies as she waits for me to answer. I don't know what to prioritize at the moment. That wouldn't make me sound selfish. My purpose for coming here to this foreign land is to get an army to fight King Outher. Which would hopefully free Alex and get my throne back.

"Even you don't know what to do. Now, we are here to gain an alliance. In doing so, we will have more firepower to fight my father with. The courts will deal with their own problems while you focus on yours."

"It doesn't matter, Morgan. If Tori and Diliha are in trouble, I am honor bound to help them."

"Yeah, well, it doesn't seem like they are holding the same standards for you." Clenching my fist, a growl of aggression bubbles in my throat.

"If I allowed them, they would be here fighting by my side, just as you are."

"Whatever you need to tell yourself." She moves to turn, and I have to swallow my anger at not cause a scene, but that pull from below is calling to me. The power that fueled my anger when Mordred threatened Alex resurfaces.

"Calm down, Gwen." Mordred's whispers fill my ears. "Remember to control your emotions. Morgan is on your side; she is not your enemy." Closing my eyes, I breathe deeply while fighting for control. *1, 2, 3, 4, 5, 6, 7, 8 ,9, 10.* "Are you in control?"

"For now." Opening my eyes, I close the distance as I continue to follow Morgan's path along the side of the building. When we reach the end, I see her pull out a map before turning towards us. Using a flashlight, I can see the layout better. The path to the palace intertwines throughout the city, making a quick covert operation a little less desirable.

"We are here." Morgan points a gloved finger at our location on the backside of the blue house, which is parallel to a row of other tall buildings. It appears the entire city is made from the same style and type of structures. The only unique part is this row of rainbow buildings. "Since flying is out of the question, I suggest we use speed potions."

"Great idea. Where do you suggest we get those?" Mordred asks, crossing her arms.

"Here." She points at a building three streets over. "There is an apothecary house here. I'm sure we can find what we need inside it."

"I don't know if you realize this, but I'm sure they are closed." I comment and they both glance at each other before snickering.

"Don't act so innocent, Gwen. Of course, we realize they are closed. But that isn't an issue." Morgan states, rolling the map back up and putting it inside her jacket.

"Are you seriously suggesting we break in and steal from them?"

"Unless you have some potions stuck up your tight ass, then yes, that's exactly what we are suggesting." Morgan states. Rolling my eyes, I sigh before gesturing for her to continue down our path of breaking laws.

Not that I wasn't breaking them anyway by landing in another court's territory without invitation. Yeah, that's grounds for war. I know that if any other royals showed up in Sagittarian Court unannounced, then the Lord Regent would surely go to war, even though I wouldn't. I just pray that Lance shares the same sentiments when the time comes for us to meet.

The apothecary house wasn't difficult for an expert lock-pick to break into. Without struggling, Morgan had the door open within seconds of our arrival. Upon entering, the scent of rosemary and lilac filtered through the air. A pleasant scent that I am more than grateful for. Not that I was expecting it to smell awful, but you never know what scents others prefer.

Wooden shelves line each of the four white walls, all stocked with rows upon rows of various potions and herbs. Pulling my mask down, I venture over to the one stacked with books. Running my finger along the spines, I tilt my head sideways to get a good read on each of them. Many are stories from the old world about princesses in glass slippers and poisoned apples.

There is even one about a great beanstalk growing to the height of the stars. "Do you like to read?"

Mordred asks from beside me. "When I get the chance to, I indulge."

"Indulge? Come on, Gwen, tell me the truth. Are you a book dragon or not?" My finger stops on the one story I have always loved. Pulling it out, the golden foil that lines the spine glitters in the light.

"This is my favorite story." I open it to the title page and smile at the smooth feel of the crisp pages. "Do you know it?"

"Everyone who's anyone knows the story about the girl who fell in love with a beast." I smirk because that isn't the moral of this story at all. "It's quite ridiculous, if you ask me."

"Why's that?" I ask, looking at her.

"Because no posh princess would ever love someone that looks like that." She points to the drawing of the prince in his beast form.

"You fell in love with a beast." I tell her, and we both glance over the far side of the room at Morgan. Her back is to us, but with her hood down, you can see her shortened purple horns jutting out of the sides of her head just behind her pointed ears. Her glamor must of fell, or she isn't too concerned about her appearance.

"I'm no princess." Mordred remarks. "And I am not in love. Never have been. Morgan was a fling, nothing more." I raise a brow, giving her an incredulous look. "I care about her, but on a deeper level, we are better than friends, than lovers."

"I can understand that." Perhaps Morgan got it wrong about Alex and I. Maybe we are better than friends or lovers.

"Morgan wasn't wrong." I look up at her. "You are having doubts about what she told you. About being Alexxander's mate."

"What makes you so sure she wasn't just saying that to save your neck?" She sighs before pulling the book from my grip, flipping it a couple of pages, and shoving it back into my hands.

"Because this story is your story." Looking down, I notice the page come to life, and I watch as the beast turns into the prince after the princess confesses her true feelings for him. My eyes gloss over with the threat of tears, but I shut it down, snapping the book closed with a loud clap.

"The problem with your theory is that Alex isn't a cursed beast." I put the book back where it belongs before looking at her again. "And like you said, a princess would never fall in love with a beast."

Pushing past her, I wipe the wetness from my lashes as I walk over to Morgan, who is busy at work.

"We would pick the one house that doesn't have the potion we need." She grumbles.

"What do you mean?" I ask, squatting down next to her.

"There is no speed potion." She sighs before pinching the bridge of her nose.

"Do they have all the ingredients for one? Perhaps you could make some." I suggest and she looks at me before chuckling.

"Your faith in me is amusing, Gwen, but I don't possess magic like that." I don't know a lot about shifter magic. Just that they can transform into full dragons or partially shift, and glamor their appearance to look like humans. Not to mention the fireballs and incredible strength.

"What do you suggest?" We stand tall as she thinks further about my question. Looking down at her watch, I mimic her and notice it's nearly a quarter after midnight.

"It's going to take at least another two hours before we make it up these hills. And with all due respect, you don't look like a girl who could make it that far."

"You underestimate me. One of these days, you will learn not to." I smirk before pulling my mask back up and heading for the door.

"Where are you going?" I hear Morgan call after me.

"To meet a prince." Just as I reach for the doorknob, it bursts open and a flood of soldiers charge in, surrounding us. Looking around, I wasn't prepared for this to happen and soon the three of us have our backs to one another.

"Now, now, I don't know about yours, but thieving is punishable by imprisonment in my Court." I look towards the man who spoke, and my stomach tightens.

"What do you mean? We are from here." Morgan speaks before I do.

The man at the front is adorned from head to toe in green leathers. A sword is sheathed on his right hip, but that is the only weapon visible. Not that he isn't hiding any other weapons. I itch to bend down and retrieve my daggers, but something tells me to stay still.

Reaching up, the man drops his hood to reveal a handsome man underneath. Charcoal hair brushes the tips of his pointed ears and darkened eyebrows. His amber eyes show mischief, but I am not afraid. A white scar runs along the right side of his face, cutting through the darkened pigment of his skin.

"Lying to me will only add to your punishment. Seize them and ensure they are thrown into the dungeons until the prince is ready to speak to them." I think about fighting, trying to escape, but I cooperate and the other two must follow suit because they give themselves over just as easily.

We are rushed outside and pushed into a square cage sitting on the back of a carriage. Four black stallions pull forward as the caravan moves. The space between us is silent except for the trotting of the horses' shoes against the stone of the road and clinking of the metal chained around our wrists.

"Well, at least we don't have to walk." Mordred remarks.

"Only we are going to be locked in the cells where I can't access my shifter." Morgan growls. "This was not supposed to happen. How could they have known we were inside?"

"Silent alarm?" Mordred guesses.

"Or you have a whistleblower amongst your crew."

"Never. None of my crew would ever betray me." Being taken prisoner is one thing I can handle. What I cannot is these two starting a bickering war.

"Enough." I bite out. Letting my voice be heard. "It doesn't matter how they found out; we are getting to where we need to go. I'm sure once the prince finds out he has me in his dungeons, this will all be sorted out. In the meantime, I would like to know why a shifter is working for him."

Mordred scoffs, catching my eye. "What?"

"Not all courts hate shifters, Gwen." Morgan states.

"How? When King Outher invaded our lands, he didn't just go after my court, he wanted all courts. There are shifter gangs in every territory." I snap back.

"Tell us how you really feel, why don't 'ya?" Mordred snarls, narrowing her eyes at me.

"I think everything is bullshit. Complete and utter shit. No one knows the truth about what really brought on this war between us. You told me that story about the blood feud, but the funny thing about it, it's a story. Just like all the books back in the shop. Each one manipulated by every tongue that ever spoke them into existence until one person finally got the gall to record and publish it."

"Every person in this world would rather lie than speak the truth. If you truly want to know what I think, then buckle up because shit's about to get real." I clench my fists as the anger inside me boils over. "Every human and shifter that walks around this world is guilty. There is no innocence anymore. So, let's stop pretending that you and I are friends because we are not."

"That's where you're wrong, Gwen." Morgan speaks so softly, I almost let my temper go, but I reach out and grab hold of that power inside of me, allowing it to weave its way into my veins and turn me into the monster I once feared. "I am your friend, and Alex is your mate."

At the sound of his name, my vision goes red. Every emotion inside of me turns completely opposite. Getting to my feet, I look down at the iron linking my wrists together and growl. Ripping them apart with ease.

"Shit, she's losing control." My head snaps at Mordred and Morgan.

"You two are my enemies and I will destroy you before you get the chance to do the same to me." Curling my fingers, I feel the essence of my power pour out of my body and into the palms of my hands. Pink lightning forms along my fingers as I smirk and aim them at the two defenseless prisoners before me.

"Guards," Mordred calls out.

"Gwen, listen to me. You don't want to do this. Control your anger." Morgan pleads, but I cock my head, all her words melting in the heat of the air before they reach me.

"Every word that leaves your mouth is a lie." I growl. "And at this moment, just like before, you will say anything to stop me from killing you and your precious whore." Releasing my power, it reaches its target as I feel my lightning strike through Mordred's heart.

"No!" Morgan Exclaims as she holds the limp body of the pirate captain. "You killed her."

"I know." I smile before turning my back to her, gripping the cage door and pushing my power into it. With a blast of magic, the door is flung off its hinges, causing the caravan to halt in its place.

"The prisoners are escaping." I hear one man yell, but I am not afraid.

"What do you think you're doing?" The man in green walks up to me. Eyes widened with fear.

"Exactly what your men said, escaping."

"I can't let you." Reaching up, I pat his face with a smile, letting my lightning prickle against his skin.

"That's cute. You think you can stop me?" I laugh before

snapping my hand out to grip his wrists. The tip of his dagger hangs in the air above my heart. Sweat pools on his forehead as he uses all his strength against me, but somehow, the power that lives inside of me is strong enough to keep a shifter at bay.

"You're not human." He growls.

"Your mistake. And now," I flip his wrists, aiming the dagger at his chest. It plunges inside him with a satisfying sound. I feel the slowing of his heartbeat through the blade. "It's your death." I whisper, as his heart comes to a complete stop.

Wiping my hands down his shirt, I look around and see the guards backing away with expressions of fear. "Now, does anyone else want to try their luck?"

When none of them speak, I step over the dead shifter and make my way to a horse. Reaching for the horn of the saddle, I stop when the familiar scent of ash and fire washes over me, followed by a thunderous voice.

"I will fight you." Letting go of the saddle, I turn around and face my challenger. "Unless you would rather come willingly, princess."

"Princess?" the guards murmur amongst themselves as I reach for my hood and mask, taking them off to reveal my identity.

"It's the fugitive." Someone states.

"Alexxander Penddragon, you look rather well for someone who was taken prisoner." I look over my shoulder to see Morgan cradling Mordred's lifeless body, tears streaming down her face. "I knew your sister was lying. There is no way I could ever be your mate."

Bending down, I retrieve my daggers and square up to him.

"Last I heard, you put a spell on me to make me believe we

were. So, tell me, princess, are we mates or not?" Alexxander smirks while holding his sword out. We circle each other and I let my power dance along my blades before engaging.

"I would never be with someone like you." I growl while my daggers connect with the blade of his sword. He pushes me backwards with incredible strength, but I do not falter.

Spinning on my heel, I plunge my daggers towards his back. He is quick and blocks them, knocking my hands sideways. I notice he doesn't strike me, and I can use that to my advantage.

"Alexxander," I sing-song, "if this is going to work out, I am going to need you to fight back."

"But I enjoy watching you dance around, princess. It's quite arousing if I didn't know what a nasty human you were." And this is where I have my advantage. Summoning my power, I let it crackle along my body, flowing into my blades as my lightning zaps from me straight towards him. Penetrating the walls as he is knocked into the building behind us.

Smoke bellows out from the debris and I keep my daggers at the ready, watching and expecting his next move. "Looks like I won this one. Now run along and play soldier somewhere else before you get yourself killed."

Strong arms wrap around me so fast; I don't realize what's happening until something sharp stabs my neck. My body shakes as my daggers fall out of my hands, clinking on the impact of the stone ground. Two large golden wings wrap around us as I feel his mouth next to my ear. "I. Win."

ALEX

"Alex?" Morgan's voice comes from behind me, but I don't look at her. Instead, I am entranced by the woman I have cradled in my arms. The serum Lettie concocted seems to work, rendering the princess unconscious. A confusing thought crosses my mind while looking at her and the hole in the fabric of my shirt. If she is human, how does she have power? And lightning? That isn't shifter power.

"Hands up, shifter." Out of the corner of my eye, I notice the circle of guards with pointed spears aimed at us. "She is our prisoner."

"No, she's mine. And unless you want to perish by fire, then I suggest you all run along to your prince and report what you saw today. Princess Gwen of Sagittarian Court is an enemy of your prince, but I am not."

"Who are you?" One of them asks, and I finally turn around to tell them.

"I am Alexxander Penddragon, son of Outher Penddragon and the Mafia King of Sagittarian Court." I look around and see my sister, bound by chains, to an iron cage. Her appearance is baffling. "Release my sister and I will spare you the death you all deserve."

Without hesitation, one guard rushes over to her and does what I say. "Her too." Morgan growls, gesturing to the woman in her arms. I watch as she carries herself and the woman over towards me.

"Who is she?" I ask softly.

"She was the love of my life." Morgan's eyes are red and

swollen from crying. My heart breaks for my dear sister. "And Gwen killed her."

"Do not fear, Sister, the princess will get her dues." Morgan's eyes flash over purple and her violet wings burst from her back as she takes on her partial form.

"Lead the way, brother. I will carry Mordred; she deserves a proper burial." I flex my wings with a nod of understanding as we take flight and head toward Sagittarian Court.

Fumes permeate the air as we light the funeral pyre for Mordred. Morgan insisted on performing it in the Fields of Camillian, but I thought it was foolish to do it so close to the wall. Lettie informed me of my father's intentions and although I somewhat believe her, something tells me there is more to this story than she was telling me.

"May the gods welcome you with open arms." Morgan sends a last prayer before turning to face me. All the lightheartedness I am used to seeing has been replaced by the vengeance icing over her heart. "That pink princess deserves to die. I don't care if she is your mate."

"Morgan, she isn't my mate." I grumble.

"What?" She scoffs.

"Lettie told me about the spell." She raises an eyebrow before shrugging, but I catch the doubt in her eyes before she masks it. "What do you know?"

"Nothing. What Lettie said is true." She pushes past me,

clearly done with a conversation. We take flight, making our way back to the underground bunker I have the princess locked away in. One of my casinos inside Walloon City is buzzing with the influx of customers.

As we walk through the glass doors, we glamor our appearance before walking through the crowded lobby. Every slot machine, card table, and bar stool is occupied by a customer. I pay little attention to them because they are all ignorant of the war that is happening outside these walls.

Approaching the back wall, I grip the door that leads into the stairwell. Morgan follows me and locks the door before we descend two flights of spiraling metal steps until reaching the next metal door and entering the room. "Well, isn't this delightful? The shifter prince and his little guard dog paid me a visit."

Flicking on the lights, the room illuminates and Morgan snarls at our prisoner. Bound by chains at her wrists and ankles, a large chain wrapped around her waist and neck, secures her to a metal table, making her completely immobile.

"I wouldn't recommend pissing my sister off. She did just send her dear one to the gods." I state while taking my suit jacket off and hanging it on the back of the chair that sits in front of the desk, littered with various devices.

"She asked for it." She snarls. "That bitch attacked me as soon as I stepped foot on the deck of her ship. And she threatened-"

Her words are cut off as if she doesn't want to mention whoever the pirate captain threatened. A weakness she doesn't want me to know about, but I will get it out of her soon enough.

"No one deserves to be killed in cold blood. Mordred was helping you." Morgan growls, her fists clenching and unclenching. If I don't make her leave, then I may not get the information.

"Sis, I think it's best I do this on my own." She stops pacing to look at me. "It isn't up for debate."

"Make her pay." She growls before pushing out of the door. Once it clicks, I roll my sleeves up to my elbows before pulling the chair out and placing it in front of her. I take my seat and watch. My eyes trail down her body, starting with the dark color of her hair. A mix of chocolate and gold, making it a beautiful bronzed blonde tone.

"Are you going to eye-fuck me all day or get on with it?" She grumbles. I like her spirit. Getting to my feet, I approach her, my eyes trailing the curve of her breasts, down her torso, and between the thick thighs. My mouth waters and my cock stirs as something flashes in my head. A memory of her thighs wrapped around my head. Her moaning my name as her release drips on my tongue.

"You're quite the enchantress, aren't you?" I growl as I snap out of my trance.

"Is that what you think?" She laughs, mocking me.

"It's what I know. Tell me, what was your plan? Enchant me and bargain for my father's surrender?"

"What are you talking about? I don't possess the magic to enchant you. Did you drink before entering this room?" I narrow my eyes, trying to search for her lies.

"The spell you put me under to make me believe we were mates. How did you do it?" I get to the point, not in the mood for banter.

"Gods, you're an idiot. Why would I ever want to make you think we were mates? You're a fucking shifter. A monster." Her words flow so easily, I almost believe them. Turning away from her, I grab one of the sharpened blades from the table before turning towards her. Closing the distance further, with only a breath of space between us as I look into her eyes. Two pools of blue and something flickers in my mind again.

More images of her looking at me with passion as I hold her against me. Our bodies pressing together under the spray of water. Shaking my head, I bare my teeth before gripping her chin.

"No more lies, princess. I know you spelled me."

"Why? Because that's what your grieving sister told you?" I nod my head, trying not to show anyone else, and she smiles. "It's funny because she's the one who told me you were my mate." I take a small step back, releasing her. "I know, it's difficult to hear the truth about one's closest friends lying to you. But I'm not surprised because clearly she lied to me, too."

"About what?" I ask, with no bite in my tone at all.

"She told me you were being held prisoner and that she wanted to free you, but we needed Lance's army to do so. Oh, and this was after she told me you were my mate, right before I almost killed Mordred the first time."

She says it without hesitation and my brain hurts. Scrubbing a hand down my face, I can't figure out who is lying and who isn't.

Various images flash through my head of me and her. Fighting together. Embracing each other. "Listen, Alex, I understand how everything sounds and looks, but trust me, if we were mates, I feel like we would fuck right now, not arguing."

"What happened between us?" A part of me needs to hear everything from her. Something deep inside me needs her to confirm these images.

"Clearly nothing worthy enough for you to remember." She states, and I see a flash of pain cross over her face. I close the distance again before reaching up and unlocking the chain around her neck.

"For every truth, I will release a lock. For every lie, I will cut you." I stare into her eyes, showing her just how serious I am. My eyes drift to her shirt as I place the tip of the blade right above the valley of her breasts. "I have no memory of the last month, and I suspect you can fill in some gaps."

"Alright, but you have to decide at the end of this." Her eyes drift to my lips, and I have the urge to kiss her. It's so familiar that it scares me.

"I know." I whisper as I meet her eyes again. We stay like that as she confirms everything that has been flashing through my mind and what hasn't. From the night of the ball to the moment I showed up to take her from Scorpion Court three days ago.

"I don't know if we are mates or not, but what I know is that there is something brewing inside of me. A darkness that is tied to my emotions. I wasn't in control back in Scorpion Court and I'm not saying I regret killing her. I just regret the pain I caused Morgan." When I don't speak, her head falls in shame. "I suppose you don't believe me."

Closing my eyes, I take a deep breath before stepping away from her. "I need a moment."

Dropping the blade on the table, I exit the room and run directly into Morgan on the other side.

"What happened? I thought there would be some screaming." She jokes, but then her eyes meet mine and it becomes clear once again. Everything I lost comes flooding in. The moments on her balcony, the visit to Tempress City, where I sacrificed my freedom for her. Even at the moment, she called me an idiot for letting Gwen go after I told her that my dragon claimed her.

"You knew." I whisper. "And you were going to let me hurt her? Why?"

She sighs, looking anywhere other than my face. "Morgan, tell me the truth. I don't know who to believe except I keep having all these memories flash inside my head and it's confusing me. Is she my mate or not?"

When she finally looks at me, I see guilt in her eyes and that confirms it.

"You told me your dragon claimed her." I stand in my spot, frozen as a mix of emotions attacks me and she continues. "I was happy for you when you told me because I thought if anyone deserved to find their mate, it was you."

"So, what happened?" I say through gritted teeth, trying to contain my anger.

"After you were taken, I went to find her. Only when I did, I didn't recognize her. She was so full of anger and hate that I knew if I didn't stop her from killing Mordred on that ship, she'd be lost to whatever darkness was inside of her. And, when I saw Mordred, I realized I never got over my feelings for her, so I didn't want her to die."

"What made her stop?" I ask as my heart thunders inside my chest.

"You." Closing my eyes, I get a grip on my anger before turning away from her. I feel her hand grip my bicep, halting me. "I only wanted you to hurt her because she killed Mordred. Alex, she isn't normal. She's a killer and needs to be stopped."

This time, I couldn't stop what I did next. My fingers latch around her small throat, lifting her into the air as my dragon surfaces. "She's our mate and I will allow nothing or anyone to hurt her. You have betrayed me and my trust. I banish you."

"What?" She chokes out as I throw her into the back wall. Slowly getting to her feet, her eyes are widening with shock and pain.

"You betrayed me."

"She killed Mordred."

"I don't give a fuck. Mordred was not your mate. Gwen is mine." I yell back, making her cower. "Because you are my sister, I allow you to walk away with your life. Never step foot into my territory again."

"You'll regret choosing that bitch over me." Without thinking, I throw a fireball at her, but when the smoke clears, she's gone and my heart breaks with her betrayal.

Turning back towards the door, I grip the knob, but I hesitate as I look at her through the glass. She's my mate. How could I have forgotten that?

"Alexxander," my inner dragon calls to me as I close my eyes and face him. *"The full moon is tonight."*

"I know."

"Then you know what is at stake if you do not solidify the bond."

"I'm aware."

A moment passes before he speaks again. *"You will not tell her, will you?"*

"I don't think we deserve to have a mate after everything."

"If that is your wish, but remember, once the full moon passes, you two will be cursed. Don't you think you should allow her a chance to decide?"

"If she rejects me, it won't matter."

"Then so be it." I am rushed back to the world around me

as I make my way inside.

"You know what's funny about all this?" She half-heartedly smirks as I close the door.

"Tell me." I swallow the dryness coating my throat.

"I know I deserve it." Her icy blue eyes lock onto mine and I slowly walk towards her. "Everything that you are about to do to me is justified."

"How so?" I ask, trying to maintain my composure.

"Because I let myself believe a man like you would claim me as theirs. That someone who risked his life for me, showed me passion for one kiss, and cared for me, could ever feel something other than lust for me. The Lord Regent was right. I'm a pathetic excuse for a royal and Morgan was right when she called me a killer, because that's what I am."

"No, you're not." The words leave my lips and I realize I am back in front of her. One more step and I can close the distance and have her in my arms again. She laughs and rolls her eyes.

"Get it over with, will you? Rid your world of one less human." The self-hate and loathing she has for herself pains me more than anything, and what leaves my mouth is out of my control.

"I can't do that, princess."

"Coward." She growls.

"You're right to call me one, but not for the reasons you think." I cup her cheek and allow myself to bask in the feeling of her skin. I run my thumb along her bottom lip as I itch to kiss them again.

"Stop looking at me like that." She snaps.

"Like what?" my eyes meet hers again.

"Like I'm the only person in the world." It comes out as a

whisper. "Stop giving me hope."

"Why is having hope such a bad thing?"

"Because it means there is something to fight for and I have nothing left." The pain in her eyes stabs me and pains me in ways no one should ever feel. She is wrong and I need to show her. Leaning forward, I whisper against her lips.

"You're wrong about that, princess."

"Why?" I smirk.

"Because you have me." I press my lips to hers, groaning at the soft feel of them. I break our kiss, allowing her to speak.

"Why'd you kiss me, Alex? To add to my torture. Because it won't work. I feel nothing but hate for you and your kind." Stepping further away, I turn away from her, grabbing the keys from the table before going back to her and unlocking her from her chains. I catch her as she falls forward. "You just fucked up, releasing me."

A knee to my gut comes before I see it, but I ignore the pain, gripping her ankle and pulling her to me. We roll across the floor until I have her pinned beneath me. "Calm down, princess. Let's talk about this."

"Why? So you can tell me more lies?" She strains against me.

"As I've told you before, I have never once lied to you and if I remember correctly, I swore I never would." She pauses a moment before sighing.

"What could you possibly say to me I don't already know?" Looking at her beneath me with all that pain and anger, I know without a doubt that I need to tell her.

"You're my mate, princess and I choose you."

CHAPTER 12

GWEN

YOU'RE MY MATE, PRINCESS, and I choose you.

His words steal the breath in my lungs as I look deep into his blue eyes. His glamor disappeared, showing me his truest self while speaking it. I know Morgan said it, but I didn't believe it until I heard him speak it. But how can I be sure this isn't some trick?

"Princess, did you hear me?"

"Get off me." I say without the bite I had intended, and he cocks a brow but does what I say, helping me to my feet. Our hands stay connected, but reluctantly, he releases me. Palming my face, I try to figure out what I am supposed to do now. How can this be? He is a shifter. I'm a human. But then again, no human I know can shoot lightning through their fingers.

"Okay, so this wasn't the reaction I was suspecting." I snap my gaze to him, catching the sight of his beautiful golden wings. They shimmer against the light, making him even more mesmerizing than the first time I ever laid eyes on him. "Look, I know that a lot of shit has fucked up this last month, but I don't want to fight this. You were taken from me for three weeks and it broke me."

"What does that even mean?" I ask, trying to keep my emotions in check.

"It means that you walked out on me and I was too stupid to stop you when I had the chance. Then, when Morgan smacked the sense back into me, you were gone. I searched for you for days and the closer I got, the further you drifted until you were completely gone."

"You were sleeping when I left. And just so you know, no one stops me from doing what I want." I cross my arms, eyeing him.

"Don't I know that? But, trust me, princess, I would've done whatever it took to make you stay with me."

"Then why didn't you?" I ask, uncrossing my arms as he scrubs a hand down his face. Somehow, in the mists of our words, we got closer. His fiery scent washes over me, causing a shiver to run down my spine.

"Because I was afraid."

"Afraid? What could scare you?" He smirks before reaching out and tucking a loose strand behind my ear. His fingers run along my jaw as he grips my chin, making my throat go taut.

"Losing you." I swallow hard as tears swell in my eyes. "If I lose you, then I lose everything. There is no life worth living that doesn't have you in it."

"How could you possibly say this? We spent a week together. Just because you say I'm your mate doesn't mean that you automatically love me." I don't deserve to be loved. That's what I want to say.

"No, but it means if you deem me worthy enough." I sigh, looking away from him, but his grip on my chin tightens. "Don't look away from me, princess. Look into my eyes as you reject me. That way I know you mean it."

As I stare into his eyes, I see the truth behind everything and my heart thunders in my chest. "What happens if I do?"

"If you reject me, then you will be free. You'll never have to see me again." Should I reject him?

"And if I don't reject you?" It comes out huskier than I intended, and I see his eyes alight with desire.

"Then you'll be mine forever and I yours. We'll have our entire lives to fall in love although, I don't think it will take long for me to know." The tears fall and I do nothing to stop them. "If you give me the honor of being your mate, you will know nothing but love, nothing but loyalty, because I will devote every day of my life to making sure you know just how much you mean to me."

"You can't say things like this." I croak as a sob erupts, and he wipes my tears away. "I don't deserve any of this, Alex. I'm a killer, a monster. There is darkness inside of me I cannot control."

"I'm a monster too, baby. I've killed more people than you, I assure you. But you don't deserve to go through any of this alone. I'm here and I'm giving myself to you. Accepting all the good and all the bad." He smiles at me, and it breaks me. Breaks the restraint I was holding onto as I allow myself to give into the chemistry between us.

"Then claim me, Alex. If I'm your mate and you accept me for everything I have done, then prove it. Show me I am yours and you can have me." His lips crash against mine in a claiming, earth shattering kiss, as we pour all our emotions into it.

His hands move to my hips, lifting me off the ground, and I wrap my legs around his waist, grinding against his erection as he carries me towards the table.

"Alex," I moan as his lips trail the side of my neck. "If you don't rip my clothes off and take me right now, I am going to walk away."

He growls an animalistic sound before I hear the ripping of fabric and a gust of cool air hits my back.

"On your feet, princess." He orders, those eyes darken with desire. I feel the tips of his claws run against my skin as he pulls my ripped clothes off my torso. "You're perfect."

He kisses me deeply again as I tear at his shirt and moan as I feel his heated skin. Running my hands along his chest, I pause a moment.

"Who did this to you?" I snarl as I see the scars littering his body.

"Later, princess." He lifts my eyes to meet his.

"They better be dead, because if not, then I'm going to kill them for hurting you." He chuckles before kissing me slowly.

He moves his lips down my neck, trailing the valley of my breast before clamping his mouth down on one and palming the other. My head falls back, and I moan, running my hand through his silky hair. I hear the ripping of fabric as his claws run down the length of my pants and soon I am in nothing but my boots.

"Don't fuck up my boots." I demand, and he smirks at me.

"They aren't in my way." He growls before picking me up and placing me at the edge of the table. The cool metal clashes against my heated skin. "Hold on to something, princess." I shudder as I grip his horns while his tongue runs through my soaking pussy.

"Yes," I moan as he picks up pace before inserting two fingers into me, pumping relentlessly, sending me into a blissful state of euphoria. As he sucks on my clit, his fingers move inside me in the most delicious way as I chase my orgasm. "I'm so close."

"Cum, princess. Now." He growls before biting me and sending me straight over the edge. I grip his horns, grinding my pussy against his face as I ride out my orgasm. My walls clench down on his fingers, and I moan with his name on my tongue.

I hear the unbuckling and zipping of pants, but I don't move, still coming down from my high. Alex hovers over me, placing his hand at the back of my neck before kissing me. "If you have any regrets and doubts, you need to tell me now before we go through with this."

Memory of the last time we were like this flood my mind, and I can't help asking lingering. "What if I pass out again?"

"I will not fuck you while you're unconscious, princess. I don't think it will happen this time."

"Why?" He leans forward, kissing me before answering.

"Because this is about our mating bond and not just desire." His words reassure me, and I nod my head. "Words, princess. I need to hear you speak them."

"Make love to me, mate." I mirror his smirk as he groans before I feel him push inside me. Wrapping my legs around his waist, I dig my heels into his ass, urging him further. The pace is slow at first, and my walls adjust to his size, but I need more. "Faster, Alex."

"Fuck, you're tight." He groans as he kisses me before picking up pace. The table shakes with each punishing thrust deep inside me as our eyes lock. My heart opens up to him. To us and our bond, I feel it forming into place between.

"Alex," I moan.

"I know." He kisses me deeply as we move faster. My nails scrap down his back as he sucks on-the-spot right below my ear. I feel my orgasm building again, but I hold it back, afraid it will end too soon. "Don't hold out on me, princess."

"Let go with me." I plead, telling him I want this. I need this to happen, so I know we are one.

"I will never deny you anything." He reaches between us, finding my clit. He circles it while kissing me deeply, his tongue dancing with mine as I get closer to the edge. Taking my bottom lip between his teeth, he bites down, eliciting a moan and causing my orgasm to rip through me. I feel my walls clench down on him and he follows me into bliss.

His golden wings burst to life as he fills me with his seed and magic comes to life between us. "I wanted it to last longer."

"We have the rest of our lives, Alex." I cup his cheek and he smiles at me, feeling the bond solid between us.

"Indeed, we do." As I look into his dark blue eyes, I smile a real one for the first time in a while at the pure joy I feel at knowing he is my mate. That Alexxander Penddragon chose me, claimed me, made me his.

"You're mine forever more, princess."

"And you're mine, shifter boy." He groans as I say his nickname.

"I thought after we had sex you'd realize I'm not a boy." I smirk at him.

"I think you need to remind me." He groans and I feel him harden again inside of me.

"With pleasure." He growls and fucks me hard against the

wall. We didn't spend the entire night in the cell, at some point we made it to the apartment above his casino unseen and after he feasted on me in the shower, my body was so worn out, I fell into a peaceful sleep curled against his chest.

My mate.

My heart.

My soul.

Alexander Penddragon was mine from the moment we laid eyes on each other, and I don't regret a single moment between us.

I wake up with Alex's mouth on my pussy. Licking and teasing me into an early morning orgasm. I grip onto his horns and ride his face until I am clenching around his fingers and screaming his name. When he lifts his head, I smile at his swollen lips covered in my juices.

"Good morning, princess." He crawls up, licking his lips, before kissing me deeply. "Are you too sore to go again this morning?"

I am, but I feel as though the pain is worth it when I feel the tip of his cock rubbing against me. "Maybe, but it will be worth it."

"I do not wish to hurt you, princess."

"Haven't you heard there is a fine line between pleasure and pain?" I run my hands down his back, purposely running them over his wings before wrapping my legs around his waist. "If you don't fuck me, then I'm going to do it myself."

He growls before thrusting inside of me. The wince of pain turns into a moan of pleasure as I kiss him. "This pussy belongs to me, princess. You don't get to touch it unless I say so."

"Prove it." He takes me on a challenge and pulls out of me as I whimper at the loss of him.

"Flip over, princess. On all fours." I do as he says, the anticipation making my pussy wet. I don't get any warning as he thrusts inside of me, pumping in and out as the headboard cracks the drywall. His hand grips my hair, tugging me against his chest. "Touch yourself. Milk my dick. I want to hear you scream my name as you pleasure yourself."

I run my hands over my hardened nipples, pinching them before snaking a single hand down my body until riding my throbbing clit. I add pressure, just the way I like it, and moan as I rub it, matching his pace. My orgasm builds until I can no longer hold on to it and scream his name. It's muffled as his mouth claims mine and he follows me into bliss.

We slump down onto the mattress into tangled limbs, and he gently pulls out of me before kissing me softly. We stare at each other in silence for a while, but I sigh, knowing we will need to leave this room soon.

"What's on your mind?" He asks as he runs a hand down the length of my back.

"There is a war brewing, and we need to stop it before it's too late."

"I know." He states. "My father has an army of soldiers that is no match for your human armies."

"Perhaps if we got all the courts to join us, we would win." He shakes his head and I sit up. "Surely the number of shifters does not outweigh the number of humans."

"You're right, but my father has one thing your human

armies do not."

"What's that?" He sits up next to me before explaining how his father possesses the magical relic that can give human shifter abilities. Only these mutated humans are unpredictable. "How did he get his hands on that? It was locked inside the Sagittarian Court vaults. There are only a handful of people who know that."

"Let me guess, the Lord Regent is one of them?" I shake my head and sigh.

"That fucking bastard. Gods, he is a traitor to not only me and my court, but to the entire world." Tossing the covers off me, I make my way to the shower, not worried he wouldn't be following, as I slip inside and wash quickly. Before he is even done, I get out and wrap a towel around myself. "Do you have extra clothes here?"

"Nothing that will fit you." I walk out into the bedroom, using my second towel to wrap my hair up. When the water turns off, he steps out moments later with a towel wrapped around his waist. "What are you plotting?"

"Your father has his hands on a relic that was under my family's protection. I need to get it back. But, to do so, we need help." He crosses his arms and leans against the wall, so I continue, "I know there aren't many people we can trust now, but we only need two. Tori and Diliha. They have other magical relics within their palaces that can help us retrieve the Golden Star."

"Look, if you think we can trust them, then I will give them the benefit of the doubt. But there is something else we need to figure out."

"What's that?"

"How the hell do you have magic and what exactly is

running inside your veins?"

"Where do you suppose we get those answers from?" I ask him and he walks over to me, placing his hands on my hips.

"The gods. They grant us all our power, so they will answer you."

"Are you suggesting we take a trip to the Temple?" He nods. "What makes you so sure they will answer?"

"Think about it. The Star was gifted by the Sun Goddess, which means the other relics are gifted by the other gods. I imagine if we take a brief trip to Valerian Court, ask Victoria to hand over hers and we go to the Temple there, summon the god and tell them what happened, we will get their help."

"That's assuming they don't smite us first. Gods are unpredictable, Alex. We need to be careful approaching them." His forehead presses against mine, giving me his strength. "But that's all we have to work with at the moment."

"We'll figure this out, Gwen. My father and Lord Regent will not get away with any of this."

"I know." I look up at him, and my body relaxes with his touch.

"My vixen." He whispers against my lips.

"What does that mean?"

"In my language, it's a term of endearment. It means my heart because that's what you are, Gwen." He doesn't need to elaborate further. I understand what he means because he's mine too. I kiss him deeply, allowing myself to feel free and safe in his arms, knowing that I already love him with all my heart. All my soul.

ALEX

The change in weather was to be expected as we flew further south, across the Black Sea. My body temperature does enough to keep me and Gwen warm.

When we awoke this morning, she contacted Victoria and Diliha and found out they were in a safe house within Valerian Court territory. I still don't trust them, but I can be cautious enough for both of us. We left under the cover of the night. My wings will be easily spotted during the day, a risk neither of us will take.

Shifting into a full dragon would have been more comfortable for Gwen, but I am ashamed to admit that he is still locked down.

"Are you able to fly faster?"

Her grip is tight around my neck and waist, and my arms have been wrapped tightly around her torso since we started four hours ago. I can feel fatigue affecting her. Whatever power she has, it isn't a constant, but I am strong enough to hold her until we get to our destination.

"We're almost there, just a little while longer." I whisper in her ear and love the feeling of her soft breath kissing my neck. Gwen has saved me in more ways than she knows, and I'm going to show her just how much she means to me, by taking down my father and getting her throne back.

We land in the tundra of Pattiken Village. It's quaint, and only has a population of two hundred citizens to include the working dogs and yaks. The igloos are made of bricked snow, compacted and frozen. I was told by one local they are well insulated as long as the fire is persistent and that can be perilous for them at certain times of the year when the lumber trade is slow.

Gwen and I dressed in thick wool coats to prepare for the snow, but it isn't enough for her by the chattering of her teeth. "Princess, if I let my wings out, we will not be so inconspicuous here."

She rubs her arms and wipes the flakes from her lashes before looking over at me to say, "Just tuck me under your arm like a normal person."

I chuckle before reaching out and doing just as she suggested. Soon after the chattering died down, we made our way to the furthest part of the village.

The Pattiken Inn is the largest igloo in the village, around twenty feet high, fifty feet, and thirty feet in width-according to the pamphlet. We enter through a curtained threshold and the temperature instantly warms as we are greeted by a large stone fire at the center in front of a large desk.

"Welcome, one room?" The villager behind the desk greets us, and I nod while Gwen continues to gawk at the architecture of the building.

She grabs my arm before whispering in my ear, "There is no way this is possible without magic, right?"

"Not everything is made with magic, Princess. Remember, there is technology and science." I press a kiss into her hair, breathing in her floral scent, before making my way over to grab the key from the worker.

"You will be thirty rooms to the left, then twenty to the right, then room number five-hundred and twenty-two is at the very back." He smiles at me, a large white one, almost too friendly for my taste.

Before I can look into it further, Gwen grabs the key, thanks the man, and runs off down the hall, making a growl leave my throat in protest. Her laughter echoes down the hall as she races down the corridor. "Princess, what are you doing?"

"Catch me if you can," she giggles again, and a smile forces its way on my face at the obvious game she wants to play.

I run forward, following the path the front desk villager orders us, because no doubt that is what she is doing. My heart thunders with the adrenaline of this chase. My inner beast is calling forward as it hunts down his prey.

"You're getting colder, Mate." She bellows down the hall and I sprint forward, tapping into my shifter magic until I see her chocolate hair whip around the last corner. "If you don't catch me, I'll have to warm myself up without you."

I growl at the insinuation and turn the corner, only to find it empty. What room did he say again? I look at the surrounding plaques, noting that I am in the five-hundreds, which, if I remember correctly, means I am close to our room. I take another five minutes before I finally find our room.

The door is cracked and my heart drops because I know she wouldn't leave it open if I wasn't right behind her. A noise comes from inside, and when I register the sounds, I burst through the door, finding my mate naked on the bed with her fingers inside her pussy.

I slam the door closed, locking it before turning around to glare at her. "What the fuck are you doing?"

She ignores me and continues to bring herself closer to an orgasm. My cock is hard as steel at the sight and scent of her arousal. I move to stand in front of her and her hooded eyes meet mine before she speaks to me. "Are you going to stand there all day, or are you going to come join me, mate?"

I shed my coat and suit jacket before rolling up the sleeves of my shirt until my forearms are exposed. My glamor falls because I am nearly tapped out on my magic, and I move to stand directly in front of her. Her eyes connect with mine and my heart swells at the connection I feel with her, my mate.

She picks up pace, using both hands this time and as badly as I want to take over, I make her wait. Depriving her of what she really wants, which is my touch, but she fucked up and ran off. This is her punishment. I smirk at her before leaning forward, placing my hands on either side of her hips, not close enough for skin to skin, but enough that my breath kisses her navel.

"Alex," it comes out breathlessly and by the buckling of her hips, I know she is close. "Touch me."

I shake my head and the satisfaction of her whimpering in frustration just about breaks me. Narrowing my eyes at her, she licks her lips seductively, but I reign in my control, curling my fingers into the comforter.

She groans and does something I wasn't expecting nor prepared for. In a matter of a heartbeat, she moved with a speed no human ever could. She has me on my back, her hips straddling me and her eyes widen with shock. Like she didn't know how that happened.

"I guess we have discovered a new power, Princess." She smiles at me before leaning in for a kiss that I dodge before flipping us, pinning her beneath me. "No."

"You would deny your mate?" She questions, feigning hurt.

"I still need to punish you for taking off and leaving the fucking door open. Anyone could've walked in and seen you, then we'd have a bloody mess on our hands."

She bucks up, grinding her hips against my cock. "You

want me too. You enjoyed the hunt."

"Maybe so, but right now, you don't deserve to be rewarded for misbehaving. If you take your punishment, then I may let you cum."

"What did you have in mind?" Her teeth come out to claim her bottom lip and I sit up, removing my belt from its loops and wrapping it around her wrists, tying them to the small hole in the headboard. The rest of my clothes soon follow, discarded on the floor, and I move back over to the side of her head.

Angling my hips, I grip the base of my cock and rub it against her lips. She opens, and I thrust in. Fucking her mouth until she is choking and tears fall. "Good girl, your mouth was made to take my cock."

She moans around me, and it vibrates through me, sending me close to the edge. I thrust in until she relaxes her throat and I pull out, coating her breasts and face in ribbons of cum.

The bed dips when I get off and go to the bathroom to get towels to clean her up, then myself. Once she is clean, I hover over her, leaving her restrained while I claim her mouth with mine, tasting the remnants of my seed on her tongue.

When I break from her lips, I move down her body, kissing and sucking along the way until my tongue darts out to taste her arousal. "Yes."

I close my mouth on her cunt, licking and sucking until I insert two fingers and pick up a fast pace until she is clenching around my fingers. I untied her while she came down from her high and pulled her into my chest, wrapping my wings around us in our own cocoon.

We lay like that for a while, soaking in each other's presence until she speaks. "We are going to meet them tomorrow."

"Are you ready?"

"I am, but I am worried that something is going to happen."

I gently grip her chin and make her look at me before planting a kiss on her lips. "Nothing will happen to you. Not as long as I am around to protect you."

"I can take care of myself."

"I know, but you don't have to."

She sighs before snuggling deeper against my chest. "Do you think Tori and Diliha will help? I mean," she interlocks our fingers before continuing. "The Golden Star was in my court for a reason, I'm sure of it. And I've been thinking about the timelines of everything."

"Timelines?"

She sits up to face me. "Twenty years ago, the war ended, my parents and the other monarchs all died, and the wall went up. The relic was born. What if it kept the peace in my court?"

I raise a brow. "I'm not following you."

"Right. Okay, when did you cross the wall?"

"Right after I turned eighteen."

"And did anyone before you cross?" I furrow my brows, trying to think, but the only memory that seems to pop up is when my mother died.

"You think that my mother got killed because of magic?"

"Yes. I mean, just think about it. You and your mom are the first ones to cross since the war ended."

"And my father warned everyone, but I didn't listen." I rub my chin, the guilt resurfacing again. Gwen's hand lands on my chest and I meet her eye. "I know, but it still hurts."

"Alex, I'm not saying a human isn't responsible for her death, but I say that if the relic did what I think it did, she was also killed with magic."

I run my fingers through my hair, exasperated by this theory because it makes the most sense. "Okay, so then speaking with the gods is most definitely the correct move."

Gwen reaches behind her, opening the drawer to the end table next to the bed and pulls out a pad and pen. "What are you doing?"

The pen moves, and without looking at me, she answers. "Taking notes, we don't need to go in there and completely forget what we want to ask them."

I chuckle and then reach out to touch her cheek. "I..," they are right there, the three words I have never spoken to someone that wasn't family, but I can't bring myself to say them because it will change things. "I think that's an excellent idea."

We continue into the night discussing topics to ask the gods and things about our past. So far, I have learned that she loves waffles covered in syrup and coffee, which I already knew. Her favorite fruit is strawberries and the least favorite is tomatoes because they just make her gag. Chocolate is a delicacy that she despises and prefers butterscotch over caramel.

"What's your favorite color?" She asks while taking another spoonful of vanilla bean ice cream, another favorite of hers.

I reach out with my thumb and wipe the corner of her mouth before answering her. "Pink."

She looks up at me, a blush rising in her cheeks. "Stop lying."

A growl rumbles in my throat. "I'm serious."

She eyes me before swallowing another spoonful and then licking her lips. "We should get some sleep. Tori and Diliha will meet us in the conference room in the morning."

She moves the food from the bed, cleaning up while I put the ice cream in the freezer. We are soon tucked next to each other, my wings wrapping around us, adding an extra layer of warmth. I soon hear Gwen's soft breathing, telling me she is asleep, and I let myself fall soon after.

CHAPTER 13

GWEN

"**S**TOP FIDGETING," ALEX PLACES a comforting hand on my right leg underneath the table in the Inn's conference room, he gives my knee a quick squeeze. My entire body feels on edge, a bead of sweat rolls down my face as my eyes constantly dart around the room. I don't know why I am so nervous.

Getting to my feet, I pace before checking the clock on the wall. "They are five minutes late. What if something happened to them? What if-"

"Nothing happened. I'm sure they will step through those doors any second." Alex states while pushing to his feet and coming close to cup my cheek. I lean into his touch, something that seems to come so easily to me since I accepted the bond between us.

A few seconds later, the doors open and I rush over to embrace my two best friends. "Gods, I've missed you both so much."

Diliha pulls back at the same time Tori does and says. "We've missed you too, but there is something we need to tell you before we get down to business."

"Okay," it comes out as a nervous stutter and my anxiety increases as my two best friends look at one another before one of them finally speaks.

"Gwen," Tori starts before interlocking her fingers with Diliha's. "Diliha and I are together."

I raise a brow, unsure of what she means, and then I look at their joined hands once more, before remembering how long they have been staying together and how supportive they both have been about me and Alex. It clicks, "Before I jump to conclusions, you mean in a romantic relationship, right?"

"Yes," Diliha answers and they both give me a worried look before a smile cracks across my face and I embrace them again.

"That's amazing. I'm so happy for you."

"You're not mad?" Tori asks as I step back to give them their space.

"Not at all. Why would you even think that?" Tori rubs her arm nervously before answering, "Because we are two women and we're supposed to marry princes."

"You want to get married?"

"No, I mean, maybe, we haven't talked about it, it's just, this is all still new, but it feels right, you know?" Diliha blushes.

"Yes," I look over my shoulder towards my mate. "I understand more than anyone."

Tori and Diliha look over and see Alex leaning against the wall, watching us. "He's smoking hot, girl."

"Thanks, I guess."

"Well, are you going to introduce him or what?" Tori asks and I gesture for my mate to come closer.

"Tori, Diliha, meet Alexxander Penddragon, my mate."

They both stop their ogling to snap their heads towards me again. "What? Mate? Explain."

We move our little group to the table, and I give them a synopsis of everything, including the lineage that I may have shifter blood. "So, it's possible, right?"

They look at Alex, who's been silent this entire time until now. "It is, but no shifter has lightning power."

"Okay, so I assume you are meeting with us because you need help to find out how you have this power?" Diliha asks.

"Yes, but there's more." I answer her before looking at Alex for support. "The Golden Star is in the hands of King Outher. He's been making an army of humans with shifter abilities. We don't know how, but we believe it is the relic that was locked in my vaults, last I heard. Only, I think Warren has something to do with Outher getting his hands on it."

"How can we help with that?" Tori asks.

"Well, we know you each have your own relics for your Courts, so we wanted to borrow one to go to the Temple of the gods here to speak with them." I answer quickly.

The room goes silent for a moment. Tori blows out a breath and leans forward. "Well, if you think it will help, then I will lend you mine."

Alex speaks, his voice laced with suspicion. "Just like that?"

She shrugs her shoulders, and Alex leans in to whisper in my ear. "We need to speak in private."

"Why?" His eyes narrow at me as if he is trying to say *don't fight me on this*. I nod, and then we get to our feet to create some distance.

Once we are on the other side of the room, a good enough distance to where we won't be heard, he speaks. "I don't trust it."

"What? And why? Tori just offered us exactly what we wanted."

"Yeah, a little too easily."

"She's my best friend. There isn't anything we wouldn't do for each other." I raise a brow. "I know your only friend was Morgan, but those two would do nothing to hurt me."

Alex moves closer, placing his hands on my hips and looking deep into my eyes. "I wouldn't be saying this if I didn't feel that you didn't need to hear it, but think about this for a moment. Your Golden Star was protected at all costs, correct?" I nod.

"And you, Warren, and maybe one other person only knew about its existence, correct?"

"Besides the other monarch, yes."

"And if your friends wanted to use it, wouldn't you want to know the risks more than anything?"

"Alex, I don't understand what you are trying to say."

He ruffles his golden locks before answering me. "I'm saying that Victoria is giving up her kingdom's power source and risking it being lost or stolen, for you. Just because you suspect the gods can answer your question and that's if they show their face."

I huff a sigh, shrugging him off. "I'd do the same thing for her."

"Gwen, please just trust-"

"No." I step further from him. "No, you're my mate, but that doesn't mean you're the only one I trust. This is my power, my kingdom, and my choice."

I don't let him speak any further before I join my friends at the table. "Is everything okay?"

"Yes, let's get started."

Alex remains in his spot for the rest of our meeting. We concluded Tori would take her leave to fetch the Frost Crystal, and meet us at the Temple within Valerian City-a single day's ride from here.

Back in our room, the silence between us is almost suffocating, but I don't need to be the first to say anything. Alex was the one who disagreed with me, not the other way around.

I sat up reading one book provided by the Inn. It's a romance about two enemies that rely on one another to save the world. "You know the problem with reading those books of yours is that it's unrealistic."

"No shit." it comes out sharp, not like I intended it to, but he just insulted my book. No one insults my books and expects me to be sweet about it.

"Are you mad at me, Princess?" I flip to the next page, ignoring him. Not that it helps me stay focused on the words. The bed dips and I turn over, not wanting to face him. "Are you seeking a punishment? Is that why you are choosing to ignore me?"

The audacity that he thinks that is why? Instead of answering him, I snap my book closed and get out of the bed, slipping on my shoes and exiting out the door. Let him stew for a minute until he is groveling at my feet.

I make my way towards the front desk area, deciding to take my reading out onto the covered and heated patio. Upon entering, the smell of pine welcomes me as does the star covered sky. There are cushioned chairs spread out across the vast space, all vacant, which are inviting.

No people means no chance of socializing and I can really get lost in my story. I nuzzle into the spot at the far-right corner, the perfect vantage point for me to see anyone coming and going from this space, as there are no windows and one exit. The glass frame leaves the surrounding area in perfect view, and I admire the landscape of this land.

The snow is a glistening bed of pearls, making the village look particularly beautiful at night. I haven't visited Valerian Court in quite some time, and I am excited to see it again. To know what has changed in the last five years.

One hundred pages and a couple logs on the fire later, I am so attuned to the book that I barely notice someone speaking to me until the shadow cast over my page and my hand instinctively moves to the dagger in my boot.

"Hello," I look up and see a man dressed in a white long-sleeve, black pants and boots. Once I realize he isn't presenting as a threat, I relax.

"Hello."

"Good book?"

I can't see his face. "Yes."

He tucks his hands into his pockets, and the movement makes me uncomfortable. My fingers kiss the hilt of my dagger, reassuring me I am not defenseless in case the man attacks.

"So, this is awkward." He comments and I nod my head, not breaking eye contact. "Do you mind if I sit with you?"

"Excuse me?"

"Well, you seem so serene, and I have had a terrible day. Just figured I could sit with someone without talking to them for a while."

"People do that?"

He smirks at me, rubbing his chin before moving to the chair across from me. "Are you an introvert?"

I close my book, unsheathing my dagger just a touch as I cross one leg over the other to block it from view. "Only to strangers."

He leans forward, resting his elbows on his knees, as I catch dark curls casting a shadow over his face. "Are you from the city?"

"No." I answer, scanning his delicate features. The beams from the moon are almost bright enough to reveal his entire face. He is handsome and doesn't appear to be Fae, but I wouldn't know if he was using a glamor or not.

"Are you afraid?"

I pull my dagger out, keeping the cool metal pressed against the fabric of my pants. "Why would I be?"

"You are alone with a stranger with no one around to hear you scream."

I couldn't help but chuckle at his words. "You clearly think someone isn't listening."

He rubs his hands together, his smile faltering as he narrows dark eyes at me. "You shouldn't have left your room, Highness."

I push to my feet, bracing both of my daggers into a fighting position as I stare at the stranger. "Who are you?"

He casually gets to his feet, seeming unfazed by my weapons, and speaks. "A messenger."

His glamor falls to reveal two black horns twisted up on either side of his head above two pointed ears. Two crimson eyes narrow at me while black wings burst from his back and a ball of flames forms in his hands.

"You don't want to do this." I exclaim as I try to reach for my power. He charges forward, but I spin out of his reach, catching his backside with the tips of my blades.

I face him again, my heart thundering in my chest as he launches his fire at me. Falling to the floor, I use the large couch to cover me, but soon it is engulfed in flames and the heat kisses my skin. Pushing to my feet, I look around for my attacker, but I don't find him quick enough as a blast of flames sends me flying into the glass with a crack.

My vision blurs and I am sure my body should be on fire. It should hurt, unless the pain is so bad I have become numb to it. A large frame stands over me, two boots coming close to my face, and I hear murmurs. "She should be dead."

The voice is female, but I don't recall anyone else being in the room. "The flames didn't hurt her. What do we do now?"

As my vision clears, one of their faces comes into view. "Morgan?"

"Bind her. It's time my father got to meet Princess Gwen." A shot of pain and darkness hit me as her boot shoots forward, connecting with my skull and something inside of me awakens. A voice calling out, one that I don't recognize as my own as it echoes inside the darkness of my mind.

Alex, help me.

ALEX

The door closes, and I scrub a hand down my face, trying to figure out if I should go after her or not.

Instead, I decide it's best to give her space and indulge in the complimentary whiskey while scrolling through the Constellina news.

"Breaking News: The search for Princess Gwen is still on, with reports of the original story being false. She, in fact, was kidnapped by none other than Alexxander Penddragon. Lord Regent Warren speaks on the matter."

"We are all in distress over her disappearance. We urge anyone with news to contact the royal hotline immediately."
My fists curl tightly around my phone as the story continues.

"Do you think she was taken because of the war?"

"Honestly, we believe the Penddragons created the original story hoping to cover up her kidnapping. I, for one, do not know their intentions because we have yet to receive a ransom note or demand from King Outher or his son."

"What does this mean for the princess's upcoming coronation? Since her birthday has come and gone and she is now of age to become queen?"

"By the laws set in place by her father, King Robert, if she is to pass away or abdicate by the age of twenty-four, then the crown falls to me."

In a fit of rage, I send my phone flying across the room and it cracks against the hard wall into shattered pieces. "Fuck!"

Running my fingers through my hair, I instantly think of Gwen and know I need to tell her because she has no phone at the moment. I charge out the door, sprinting down the hall as my heart slams against my ribs.

I make it down the first hall and turn the corner. The hairs on the back of my neck raise as the lights flicker. "What the hell is going on?"

The smell of smoke permeates through the air, it isn't the usual pine scented one from the persistent burning wood, it's of burnt fabric. I pick up my pace, sprinting forward until I see the lobby doors come into view. "Gwen!"

There is no answer, and the place goes pitch black, but that doesn't inhibit my ability to see in the dark as I call upon my dragon and my eyes shift into slits.

I halt in my steps as the scent of another shifter hits me, ash and moonflower. Letting my glamor fall, my talons elongate as I look around for it. "I know you're here."

No answer. I creep forward, "Did my father send you?"

I look side to side, keeping my mind on Gwen and praying to the gods she is safe. A flash moves in the corner of my vision, and I swiped right. Only no one was there. My chest rumbles with the growl vibrating through me, and I noticed movement out of the corner of my other eye.

I swipe, my growl reverberating louder with my frustration. "Stop playing games and reveal yourself."

"But I'm having so much fun watching you." A deep male voice permeates through the air and I freeze, recognizing it. As the lights flicker on, the body attached to that voice came into view. His hands tucked deep into the pockets of his black pants, as he leans against the door frame.

He takes in my paralyzed state, moving closer to stand in front of me. "Hello, Brother."

"Arthur? What the fuck are you doing here?"

He saunters over to me, meeting my eye before smirking. "Do I need a reason to come meet my baby brother?"

A growl rumbled in my chest in warning. "With you, there is always a reason. Tell me, did father let you out and send you to do his dirty work?"

He turned his back on me, insulting me just as he always has, and answered. "Perhaps… and perhaps not."

"Don't toy with me, Arthur."

"Me? Come now, I would never."

Just as his words roll off his lips, I feel that something is wrong, and I move forward only to halt at the devilish smile spreading across his face and the soft voice echoing in my head. Alex, help me.

I spring into action, racing past my brother and through the lobby, letting my instinct guide me to her. Breaching another pair of spare doors, I find myself inside what appeared to be a patio. The glasses are littered with cracks cascading like spider webs and the furniture, if not knocked over, crackled with flames.

My heart pounds in my chest as I look for her, for my mate. "Gwen!"

My eyes search frantically as my wings burst from my back, airing out all the smoke, and the scent of blood, her blood, wafts in my nose. I track it and spot a puddle on the floor just below where the largest crack in the glass wall is.

The sound of footsteps has me turning on my heel, my talons sinking into the person's neck as my eyes go red with rage. Baring my teeth, I lock onto my reflection and realize it's none other than my brother. "Where is she? Where is Gwen?"

He gives me a Cheshire cat smile, reaching up and gripping my hand that is locked around his throat. In a twist of movements, one that I fooled myself into, he has me at his mercy, just a single flick, and he can break or dislocate my shoulder.

"Drop the theatrics, brother. Let's have a pleasant chat."

"Unless it's you telling me who took her and where, then I don't want to hear a word pass your lips."

He hums in response, relinquishing me as I fall to my knees and then push to face him. "She is gone, your mate. Captured by our darling sister. Something about revenge."

I looked sideways, my anger towards my estranged twin reseeding. "Gwen killed her lover."

"Ah, yes, Morgan might have mentioned that when she was groveling at father's feet."

"Did you come here to boast, or are you going to be helpful?"

He raises a brow at me, his eyes, like my own but different, brighter with a mix of jade and cerulean, just like our Mothers were. "Honestly, it depends on how this conversation ends."

"What is that supposed to mean? If it isn't you telling me where she is exactly, then I don't give a fuck. I can easily track Morgan's magical signature."

He shrugs, running a hand through his golden hair, as if he is pondering whether to make me beg for it. Which I would never do, not for anyone and not to him. "Seeing as you took part in our mother's death, my imprisonment, and the murder of Morgan's lover-"

"I had no hand in that."

"Ah, but you chose. What was her name again?" I didn't answer, because he already knows. "Gwen? Right, you let her go unpunished for killing our dear sister's lover because you think she is your mate."

"I don't *think*, I know my dragon claimed her."

"The dragon that has been dormant inside of you since we turned ten?"

I close my eyes, trying to get rid of the seeds of doubt he was trying to plant inside of me, inside of my soul. "I know the truth is difficult to hear, but with the very last shred of respect I have for you, dear brother, I only wish for you to think about what actually happens when you find your mate. But seeing as you nor I were alive to see the last mating ritual, then we wouldn't know. And I highly doubt father will bless you with the details, seeing how you handled his mate's death."

My brain hurts as I clutch my head, the guilt of my mother's death consuming just as it did twenty years ago, and now, because of me, my family is even more broken than it began. I did it for her, for Gwen, because she is my mate. "I felt it when we came together under the full moon. The moment I first laid eyes on her."

"Are you sure that wasn't just lust?"

I scrubbed a hand down my face, my emotions a mix of confusion, anger, doubt, and possibly regret. "Arthur, if it means saving her, then I need to do it. Gwen does not deserve to be punished or killed for my sins against our family."

He let out a sigh before closing the distance between us. "Three options, twenty-four hours."

I nod, so he continues. "Option one, walk away from this realm, this family, this life, and never come back. Option two, allow me to bring you in as a prisoner and I will convince our father to be lenient on his sentencing."

He quiets and I wait for him to continue, his eyes swirling with mischief. "And the third one?"

He leans closer, narrowing his eyes, "Option three means

that she goes to where I have been the last twenty years."

"No!" I snarl. "She would never survive that place and you know it."

"If the punishment fits." He shrugs.

"That would sentence her to death. She doesn't deserve that."

"I know a good amount of shifters that would disagree with you. Our sister included."

Arthur, the son of a bitch, has me backed into a corner. The first one would ensure I never see her again, option two means father will kill just in a less painful manner, but three, the place she would be sent to is not a place that a human princess would survive, regardless of her heightening abilities.

"Time is ticking, I shall leave you to think, but I would devise sooner rather than later because this time tomorrow will be too late."

He walks away, and my mind races before landing on one conclusion. "Wait." he pauses, glancing over his shoulder to meet my eye. "I will offer myself up to you if you promise to ensure that she isn't killed or tortured."

With a smirk of triumph on his face, he turns completely around to face me. "Is that your final decision?"

I would rather punch that smirk off his face, but if making a deal with the devil ensures Gwen is safe and unharmed, then so be it. "On a blood oath, vow to me she will not be killed or tortured, and you can hand me over to our father."

With an elongated talon, Arthur slices his right palm, and I mimic his movements before we connect our palms. "I, Arthur Penddragon, do solemnly swear Princess Gwen of Sagittarian Court with be safe from death and torture, on pain of death."

"I, Alexxander Penddragon, do solemnly swear to surrender

and become a prisoner to Arthur Penddragon." A clap of magic zaps between us, as the building trembled with the vow we took under the eyes of gods.

Two iron rings forms around my wrists, a single chain connecting them in the middle, as Arthur smirked at me, a reflection of my appearance, the only difference in our eyes and hair style. "Let's go home."

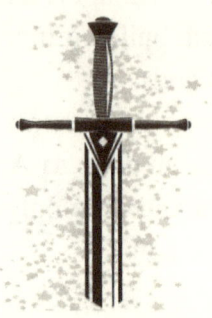

CHAPTER 14

GWEN

MY HEAD POUNDS, AND my eyes flutter open as I clutch my side, looking around to get my bearings. Red brick surrounds me on all four sides, with no windows, no doors, only a small hole in the top for breathing.

"Hello!" I exclaim. My voice bounces off the walls and back to my ears. I stand, a dizzy spell hits me and I clutch onto the brick until the room stops spinning. Running my hands along the walls, I search for an opening or hidden spot.

"They must come and go at some point," I mutter to myself. "Hello!"

"There's no use, girl." A weak male voice reaches my ears from somewhere next to me. "The guards only come when they are ordered to."

Guards? There is no way. "Where am I?"

"They call it hell, but truly, it's temporary holding until the transfer." He responds and I try to figure out where his voice is coming from.

"Transfer? What does that mean?"

"To Locknite."

"I'm not familiar with it. Where are we currently?" There is silence and then the creaking of metal hinges before the ceiling above me is opened and a gust of warm air kisses my skin.

"Hands pressed to the wall and face away," one guard orders and I do as I am told, only I will attack the moment one of them jumps down.

The brick is hot against my skin, not enough to burn me, but enough for perspiration to bead against my brow. A grunt and a thudding noise comes from behind me as boots hit the ground, my attempt to fight back turns futile as I feel something sharp against my neck. I am soon immobilized, bound by rope, and lifted into the air and out of the cage.

"Hold her head sideways," the guard at the top orders and out of the corner of my eye, I see a filled syringe coming at me just before it pokes through my skin and my body is mobile again.

The instinct to fight back pulses through me, but something else keeps me silent. *Watch. Wait. Listen. Strike.* I've heard that voice before, when I called out to Alex. He didn't come for me. I thought this whole mate bond was supposed to keep us connected, but clearly, I was wrong.

They escort me down the widening corridors until I step onto the marbled floor, dancing with the illuminated lights above. We come to a stop. I look around, seeing a single throne on a raised platform with no one else in the room. My knees hit the carpet as two firm hands push me down and I keep my eyes on the floor ahead of me. I stay like that for a few minutes. The only sound is my breathing, the buzzing of lights, until the footfalls of several more people come marching in.

When the noise dies down, I bravely look, and I am met with two dark eyes staring me down from the throne in front of me. A dark stubble lines his jaw and matches the dark curls on his head. Two large crimson wings lay laxly behind his back, and it makes me realize just who I am kneeling in front of. "So, this is the infamous Princess Gwenyfer. The killer of shifters and wielder of lightning."

I shift uncomfortably, tilting my chin up high as the room assesses me. "And you must be the infamous cold-hearted shifter, King Outher. Not very impressive if you ask me."

He laughs and the room echoes until it dies out. "Princess Gwen, you have made some enemies within my territory. Did you know that?"

I don't indulge his pointless questions with answers he already knows. "Shall I call off your list of crimes? Or should we just get down to business?"

"Do you normally engage in casual chit chat before killing your enemies? No wonder it's taken you this long to accomplish anything."

He laughs again, this time more obnoxious, and again, I wait until it dies down before hearing him speak. "You are charming. I will give you that. I can see why my son was so smitten with you."

Did he just say, was? "Do I hear trembling in your voice? Does that fact that your son will soon come for his mate and kill you have you frightened?"

His smile remains, and it unsettles me in a way that I have never felt before. Something is wrong about all this and, as if the gods were smiting me with answers, I just got mine. "Am I late?"

My ears recognize the voice, but my heart doesn't want to believe it to be him because if it were, then why is he walking in here like it's a typical day and not charging in here fighting to rescue me?

"Not at all. I was just about to deliver the princess's sentence, but since you are here, and your sister, I think you two can do it."

"Alex? What's going on?" I ask and he marches over towards me, his ash and fire scent consuming me as my eyes mist over. He kneels down to meet my eye, a look of pity befalling his face.

"Did you think I came here to rescue you?"

"That is what one does for their mate." I bite back.

"Only, he isn't your mate." Morgan's voice comes next, and I am lifted to my feet to meet both their harsh gazes.

"What does she mean? Alex," My voice croaks and my heart thunders in my chest.

Morgan crosses her arms, narrowing her eyes with a smirk on her face. "Tell her, Alexxander. Explain to the princess how you used her since the moment you took her from the palace over a month ago."

I look at Alex, trying to get a read on his face, hoping that he will tell me she is lying, that what we had and shared wasn't a lie because if it was-

"Oh, I think she is going to cry." Morgan mocks.

"Enough." Hope rises at Alex's interruption, he closes the distance to cup my cheek, and like a fool, I lean into it. Into his strength, his warmth, everything that I associated with safety and is now being presented to me as a lie. He doesn't have to speak it because I can feel it by his actions alone.

"Why?" The tears fall and my chest tightens.

"Because you were so desperate to be loved, to be chosen, that you made easy prey. All I had to do was dangle the idea that I was your mate and you jumped up, begging me to fuck you like the whore you are."

His words were venom, cutting straight through me like a thousand knives all at once. "You're lying."

"No, I'm not." His blue eyes narrow, and he leans forward to whisper in my ear. "I told you I would never lie to you, didn't I?"

"Explain yourself further." I growl, my hurt turning into rage, and I hold on to it because if this was a time for me to lose control, now would be a good one.

His lips brush against my cheek before he pulls back, his words kissing my lips as he speaks them. "Gwen, reign in your control and just know that no matter what anyone tells you, regardless if we are mates or not, it was real for me."

"That's enough, Alexxander. It's time." Outher's voice booms and as Alex looks at me, retreating to stand by his father, I swallow hard, my heart pounding in my ears as my emotions wage war inside me. "Morgan, pass your judgment."

She steps up, her cold eyes that once looked upon me like a friend would, alight with purple flames. "For the murder of Mordred Pascillo, I sentence you to death by a thousand cuts. For the enchantment used against a shifter of royal blood, I sentence you to life in Locknite. And finally, for the crime of betraying a royal, I sentence you to death by fire."

The air in the room seems to have vanished as we all wait for the king to give the order. My thoughts run rampant as I think about Tori and Diliha, praying they are still safe and out of harm's way. Perhaps after my death, they will save the realm.

With a loud bang, the throne hall doors burst open and a sound of boots hitting the floor echoed throughout the silent room until coming to a stop behind me. The scent of ash and moonflower engulf me, eliciting goosebumps along my skin and a shadow cascades from behind me. "What are your orders, Father?"

My head snaps to the deep voice and I am hit with a case of déjà vu as I look at Alex, only this time he has no wings or horns, and his right ear has a hole at the very top making it a jagged point instead of a sharpened one. "The prisoner is to spend the rest of her days inside of Locknite."

The king gets down from his throne, his wings flexing as he saunters over to me. I see no resemblances between his children and him, but that may be common for shifters. His feet come to a spot in front of me and I raise my chin up high, showing that I will not be intimidated. "Princess Gwen, I want you to take one last look at my son because, after this moment, you will never see him or anyone else again."

Narrowing my eyes at the king, I speak with words of ice. "Son? Everyone in this room is dead to me."

He smirks before nodding behind him and my world becomes dark as a cloth is draped over my head and I am dragged out of the throne hall with Alex calling my name and the last of the walls building up around my fractured heart.

ALEX

With my heart in my throat, I watched my brother drag Gwen out of the throne hall with my lies filling her ears. I would keep up pretenses about her. "Alexxander."

I turn to look at my father, wanting to punch the smug smirk off his face, but hold back. "You did well."

For the longest time, I wanted his approval, his praise, but it felt wrong. "I told you, you could trust me."

"Indeed, I will admit I had my doubts, especially when you sister came crying at my feet for you choosing that human over her. I mean, honestly, I think the entire 'mate' thing was absolutely brilliant." He chuckles, and I fake a smile.

"If that will be all, Father, I would like to turn in for the night." I need to meet Arthur in my quarters to discuss a plan. When he brought me back as his prisoner, father questioned me, and I told him it was all a part of my plan, that I told him after he contacted me when the news story broke out about us.

Arthur didn't argue it, so I can only assume he will either blackmail me or wants to help. I don't know, but I will find out soon enough.

"You may, but tomorrow we will host an event in your name. For the capture of the human princess and the downfall of the Sagittarian Court. The first of many." I bowed before leaving the room, heading down the corridors until stumbling into mine.

"Alexxander." I spin at the sound of Morgan's voice behind me. She looks different than the last time I saw her. The pink now gone from her hair, replaced with a deep charcoal color and her purple irises now a deep green. "Was what you said to father true?"

"Yes." I lie.

She crosses her arms over her chest before raising a brow. "I don't believe you."

"Wha-"

"I was there the night you told me your dragon claimed her, remember?" I swallow, worried she might betray me again. "Look, I know I acted out when Mordred was killed, but I was so grief stricken I wasn't thinking clearly, and I know what it feels like to not want to lose the person we love most in the world."

"Morgan, I don't love her."

"Right, and I didn't dye my hair green." What is her angle? "I didn't come here to fight or argue. I wanted to say thank you. I know it must have been hard to let her go. Father thought execution would be justice enough, but I disagreed."

"And why's that?"

"Because Locknite is worse than death. It's hell on earth and I don't think she will survive over five minutes."

"You're forgetting one thing, Sis." She looks away, uninterested with what I have to say. She started this and I am finishing it. "She has magic."

She shrugs. "Didn't seem to help her back there."

"And you think she won't be able to use it while in there?"

"I don't know, but what does it matter? She'll be dead before she can even try."

"Is that why you didn't tell Father?" My question stuns her. I notice the twitch in her eye, and she closes the distance between us in five strides.

"No, I don't know why I didn't tell him. All I came in here to say is that I know you lied to everyone in that room, including her. Gwen is your mate, and if I am to assume correctly, you solidified that under the full moon. You are planning something, but because I still love you, just know that you better stop and let her go because I will march to father and tell him if you step out of line."

A sharp clap makes us both flinch, and we look over to the source. Our brother. "Very well said, little sister." He kicks off the wall, smirking. "Now, I think you should scamper off and play daddy's favorite while I speak to our brother."

"Fine. But Alexxander, I swear I will gut you if you betray me again." Once the door slams shut, Arthur lets out a low whistle, and I turn away from him, needing a drink for this interaction.

"You really like to piss women off, don't you?"

"Shut it, just tell me how bad it is." I turnaround, sipping on the sweet-tasting alcohol while waiting for him to speak.

"She's a feisty one, but she hates you completely and wouldn't even look at me because we're twins." I scrub a hand down my face, cursing under my breath. "Don't feel too bad. I came here because we both held up our deal, not that I expected father to pardon you so easily after spinning that brief story."

"Yeah, well, father loves revenge and power more than anything." He nods in agreement. "Is there anything else?"

"Nope." He doesn't move to leave, and I hate the silence, so I break it.

"Arthur, what do you want?"

"To offer another deal."

"I have nothing to offer you."

"That is where you're wrong, brother." I swallow because I instantly think of Gwen and start shaking my head. "I don't want your mate, Alexxander, although I still don't think you are. I will offer my protection while she is in Locknite until you figure out how to save her."

There has to be more to this. "And what do I give you in return?"

His jade eyes gleam while a smirk forms on his face. "You'll see."

"Cut the shit, Arthur, and just tell me what you want in return."

"That is between me and your mate." He smirks before reaching out a cut palm. "Do we have an accord?"

If I can't be there with her, then I will do my damndest to protect her, no matter what. With the mixing of our blood and the clapping of magic sealing our deal, I feel like I might have made the biggest mistake of my life by letting my brother help me, again.

CHAPTER 15

GWEN

MY WORLD SPINS AS a firm hand grips my forearm, and I'm ushered out of the throne hall to what I assume is the exit.

I remain stoic on the outside, hiding the pain of Alex's betrayal deep inside, reigning in control of the mysterious power coursing through me. It didn't come when I called on it, which told me as clear as day that I had no control over it And now, any hope of learning how to control it faded the moment I was sentenced to life in prison.

The questions circling my brain made me hurt, but I want, no, *need*, to know if Diliha and Tori were safe. Did they make it out of the village? Were they intercepted on her way to get the Frozen Star? "Stop thinking so loudly, Sunshine."

I snap my gaze at my guard, then realize that it was a mistake because he looks just like Alex. Apparently, the fact he has a twin brother wasn't worth mentioning. "Who are you?"

We continue walking, my gaze returning to the floor in front of me while I wait on bated breath for his response. "Are you as deaf as you are gullible?"

"Perhaps. Or maybe I just want to know why Al- your brother never mentioned you?"

He stops, halting me in place before reaching to grip my chin, making my eyes meet his. I avert them, unable to look at his eyes. "Look at me."

"No." I growl.

"Look at me and I promise you won't see him."

"Promises mean nothing when they are spoken through the lips of liars." He moves closer to me, his body pressing into mine, causing a cascade of sensations to run through my body.

"Have I ever lied to you? We only just met moments ago, seems hardly enough time to do so, don't you think?"

He's toying with me, playing on my emotions and the harsh reality that smacked me across the face in that throne hall. "You are a Penddragon, a shifter, liar, and manipulator."

"Some advice, your Highness. If you intend to insult someone, I suggest you look them in the eye or else it will hold no venom."

"Just take me the hell away from here and stop playing around." He hums but lets go of his hold on my chin before we start moving towards double-doors and soon march out into a vast courtyard with a carriage hauling a cage sat in the middle.

At the sight, my feet stop on their own accord, my throat turns dry, and the impending fear of what this meant hits me. "Keep walking."

My guard whispers it, not harshly, but something else I can't quite describe. "I can't go in there. My people, my friends-"

He leans forward, his breath kissing my ear as he whispers.

"Don't show them your fear. Show them the princess who stood up to their king without a single ounce of fear in her words or face. You'll need that bravery to survive."

I turn my head, my eyes meeting his, and I realize he was right. Arthur Penndragon looks nothing like his brother. But I don't give myself time to analyze his appearance while someone shoves me into the cage. "Survive what?"

As the bars close on my freedom, my life, I realize I would get my answer soon enough, but Arthur's words stick with me, and everything that happened in that throne room makes my hunger to survive surge through me; because not only will I get my throne back, but I will destroy the Penddragons. And you know what they say about women.

Hell has no fury like a woman scorned.

The journey started out rough, with, zero protection from the blazing heat of the sun, and the blistering temperatures of the environment within this part of the world, had my skin blistered and lips chapped.

Water was given far and few between. I wasn't sure how many days had passed since we left the palace. We're riding further north into Dracane territory. I thought there was nothing beyond the volcanoes of this kingdom, but I have learned that is not the case.

Beyond the black volcanoes, are plains covered in ash and soot. On day one, we left under the cover of the night, and I kept my head up and eyes open, tracking the route we were taking in order for me to come back. If I escape. *Who would help you?*

When the sun rose, that's when I started feeling the thirst and hunger take over my body. By day three, I was in and out of sleep and scolded myself for not having the strength to stay awake and memorize the terrain.

"Wake up." One guard's voice jolts me awake., I sit up with the hope of water or food, but when I heard keys jingle and the hinges of the doors open, I swallowed down a hard lump in my throat.

"What's going on?" My voice cracks, and it burns to speak, but looking around, I see nothing but sand for miles around.

A hard grip on my arm makes me stumble forward, and I brace for the impact. It doesn't come. "Stop asking questions and move on."

"Where? There is nothing here." The guard smirks at me. The cage closes, and the carriage starts pulling forward. "Where are you going?"

"Shut it." The grip on my arm tightens as I hobble forward, and I'm sure that this is where I'll be stranded. In the middle of desert lands, miles and miles away from the nearest village or city, on the brink of passing out from lack of food and water.

We walk for what feels like hours and my legs are about ready to give out until we come to a halt. I look around, but see nothing except the same landscape, all sand and no hint of green. "Why did we stop?"

The guard doesn't answer me, but he doesn't have to. Once I look ahead, I find the mirage dissipates and what's revealed to me is much more than I had imagined.

Twelve narrow, round towers surround the castle in an

almost perfect circle around the incredible fortress, connected by fortified, solid walls of black stone.

Barred windows are scattered generously across the walls in an asymmetric pattern, along with holes of various sizes for archers and artillery.

A vast gate with double oak doors, a drawbridge and various artillery equipment offer a dark haven within these hot, isolated lands and it's the only way in, at least without taking down the castle walls.

Remnants of broken bones, decaying bodies, vultures and torn fabric litter the fields outside, a frightening realization of what's awaiting on the inside. The castle looks very new, but without knowing its history, it's impossible to tell if it's newly built or simply well-kept.

Fuck. I am royally fucked.

The drawbridge lowers and the various vultures picking at their meals don't appear to be phased as they continue to devour the dead.

Once the end of the bridge lands, I am ushered forward, my swollen feet screaming at me with every step I take, I have to bite the inside of my cheek to stop from crying out. *Don't show them your fear.* Arthur's words sang in my head, and I hold onto them. *You'll need it to survive.*

Survive.

That was the key word in his efforts at a pep talk. From what I witnessed outside, it doesn't appear that would be a simple task, considering from the moment I walked under that threshold, all I saw were shifters. Horns and pointed ears, some with their glamor up and others without. We are greeted at the front by a large shifter with bright green irises and cropped orange hair that shines in the beaming lights above.

"Prisoner eight-one-two ready for processing." My guard announces, and I cringe at the sound of my new identity.

The shifter looks up and eyes me from head to foot with a bored expression. His uniform is interesting and nothing that I haven't seen before. His very short-sleeved, crimson vest covers him well below his waist and is almost completely buttoned up right side. The sleeves of his black shirt are a little wide and reach down to his elbows. They're decorated with several thread linings from top to bottom.

The vest has a deep, rectangular neckline which reveals part of the majestic shirt worn below it and is worn with a small rope belt, which is held together by a decorative pin. The rope belt is a functional addition, but has some decorative value.

His brown pants are simple and narrow and reach down to his hard black leather boots. The boots are made from a fairly rare leather, but are otherwise an ordinary design.

"Eyes up here eight-one-two," he snaps, making my gaze meet his. Where I was expecting to see hate and disgust, I saw pity and it makes me want to throw up.

"Do you have her from here?" My guard asks, and the orange-haired shifter nods. "Don't worry, your Highness, I have four-hundred on you for at least five minutes."

His dark chuckle echoes even after he leaves and I'm left standing alone with my additional guard, who grips my sore arm, gentler than I expected. "Let's go eight-one-two, get sanitized, and see the medical bay before you meet your new roommate."

Medical Bay? Sanitized? Roommate? "What do you mean? I thought this was a prison."

We walk down a corridor connected to the front and approach the outside of a thick metal door. Nothing happens for a few seconds until I hear a click and the door opens automatically. I am instantly hit with frigid air that cools my skin immensely, and I don't get to stifle the groan that passes my lips without being noticed.

I catch my escort eyeing me and I don't know if he wants to hit me or kiss me by the hunger lingering in his eyes. "Is there something wrong?"

He clears his throat and looks ahead of us. There was nothing but four metal walls and another door. After a few seconds, the rushing of air fills the room and the scent of cleaner hits me, making a coughing fit irritate me. "What the fuck?"

"Sanitation, eight-one-two, don't act so melodramatic."

Once my fit dies out, the air dissipates, and the door opens. I am greeted with another blast of cold air. On the other side, I see several beds lined with ivory sheets laid out on either side of the white room. None of the beds are occupied, and that makes me nervous.

A female shifter with no hair, dressed in the same uniform as my escort, walks up to us with a bright smile on her face. "Is this our new transfer?"

"Indeed." He answers, and she looks at me with scrutiny. I more than likely look disheveled and smell like I haven't showered in five days; which is true. "Are we good?"

Her dark eyes shift behind me as she answers. "Yes, Carrigan, we are good."

"Watch her, from what I hear. She is a fighter." Carrigan states.

"I don't think we are going to have any issues, are we, dear?" From the tight grip on my arm, the domineering look in her eyes, and the sharpened tip of her canines showing, I shake my head.

The door clicks shut, and I am left alone with another shifter, again. She turns her back on me to walk over to one cart next to the nearest bed and pulls something out before turning back to me.

Silence and tension pulses between us until I decide to break it. "What now?"

She smiles at me, flashing those sharpened teeth again, and I'm curious to know if all shifters have them because Alex never did. At the thought of him, my stomach clenches and bile rises. "Hold out your arm."

I comply, because what's the use of fighting when my wrists are locked together, and I can barely stand up? I watch as she presses a needle into my arm and then shooting pain goes from the spot of the shot all the way to my neck.

"Fuck."

She chuckles. "Who knew a princess with a foul mouth?"

"You know who I am?"

"Of course. Everyone here does." She turns around and does something with the needle before continuing. "We all have bets on you. Some in your favor and others, not so much."

Bets? "What are you talking about? Why would you all be placing bets on me? You think the other prisoners are going to kill me on sight?"

She gives me an incredulous look before sighing. "Look, seeing as you are human," she winces. "I guess it's natural you don't understand what this place is. So, I will give you a brief explanation, although, you will find out soon enough."

"Locknite isn't just a prison, it's an arena, a game of survival. Only the strong survive. You look like you might put up a good fight, but you're human. They don't last after the first round."

"Round? You mean-"

"Yep. You are going to be fighting for your life everyday you spend here. So I suggest you send a prayer up to the gods to ensure you get a merciful death otherwise they will eat you alive."

"Why are you telling me this?"

She smiles, nothing menacing, more sympathetic, and I hate it. "Because it's not like you will make it past the first round. I see no harm in telling you."

"When is my first fight?" Mentally, I need to prepare and physically, well, let's just say I need food to regain some energy.

"The end of the week. Five days to prepare yourself and then the games begin."

There is no place like hell on earth, or so I thought until I was shackled inside a cage and transported to Locknite prison five days ago.

My first five days were simple, and that makes my anxiety peek because there have been no confrontations from any of the other prisoners, including my roommate.

After my visit to the medical bay, I'm pushed through a door, and handed off to another guard. I walk in silence until I'm ordered to strip bare and step into a freezing, quick shower with non-scented soap and eyes on me.

"Two minutes, eight-one-two." The guard growls while

I scrub the dirt and grime from my body. Most of it comes off, but the burns on my skin discolor the darkened pigment, turning it into a copper tone and the blisters are filled with clear liquid. The spray makes me wince, but I swallow down the tears.

Once I am done, I dry quickly and put on the new clothes. White undergarments, socks, and a crimson jumpsuit that has my number stitched above my heart. The only thing I get to keep are the boots on my feet. The corridor outside the shower stalls connects to another door. *So many fucking doors.*

On the other side, I am presented with a large square cut-out of ten levels. Each housing at least ten cells on either side. I catch the sign on the wall next to the door labeled with the number eight and then the next plaque that labels my new room, twelve.

"Rosario, you have a new cellmate." The Guard escorting me states while I look inside the illuminated four by four. A bunk bed is pushed against the back right corner, with a toilet to the left and nothing else.

The bars move with the sound of the buzzard, and I am pushed inside. When the bars close behind me, I swallow down my fear and approach the small ladder that leads up to the top bunk. A creaking sound bounces off the walls as I crawl up the mattress before letting my head hit the pillow. Not that I should call the thin material that.

My roommate does not converse, and I don't want to engage as my body calls for sleep, but my mind refuses as my senses are on high alert. *Don't show them your fear… you'll survive.*

At some point I must have fallen asleep because the next thing I knew, I was being awoken by a buzzing sound and the movement of the bars. I sit up and assess my body for any injuries, letting out a sigh of relief before getting down and looking at the bottom bunk. When I see it's empty, I peek out of the cell and see a line of other inmates standing directly outside their cells with their hands behind their backs.

When I move to the space to the left of my door, mimicking their movements, I see something to my right and bravely look. My roommate is nothing like I expected her to be. Deep brunette hair that is shaved on the sides of her head just above her pointed ears is tied back into a high ponytail. Tattoos cover her bronzed complexion from the bottom of her sleeves down to the tops of her hands.

She easily towers over me by at least three feet. Her black horns are twisted and pointed towards the ceiling, matching the long tail protruding from the small of her back. Something I have never seen on a shifter before, but also some shifters have their wings out, so it shouldn't surprise me she prefers her tail out.

Her uniform fits snuggly to her muscular frame and I can admit to myself that I am intimidated by her, not just because she did nothing on my first night, but because of how silent she is.

"Inspection time." One guard calls out and there are two that start coming down the walkway. When they step up to me, I keep my eyes to the back wall off in the distance, not giving them the satisfaction of intimidation of respect.

"Eight-one-two, our royal guest. You are as beautiful as the rumors say." The guard brushes a finger down my right cheek, and I don't flinch, despite how badly I want to punch him for touching me. "Look at me when I am speaking to you."

I refuse, holding onto my pride, but that was a mistake because his knee meets my ribs and only his hard grip on my hair prevents me from doubling over. "I said, look at me."

My misted eyes meet his flaring yellow ones, and I swallow down the pain. "Good. You know how to follow orders. Seeing as it's your first day, I will let that infraction slide, but you will look at me when I am speaking to you. Do you understand me?"

"Yes." I say through gritted teeth.

"Yes, what?"

"Sir." I snarl and he pats me on my head, adding insult to injury.

"You'll learn soon enough not to disappoint me, eight-one-two. But, I suspect by the end of the week, I won't have to look at you anymore."

"Come on, Carter. Stop wasting time." The other guard states and I add another name to my mental list of people to kill. A certain shifter prince being number two right under his father.

He lets his hold on me go before moving on and I wait until they are a suitable distance away before letting the unshed tear fall, but that is all I give him.

After thirty minutes, another buzzard sounds and the inmates turn and start walking down the corridors leading to stairs. I follow suit because I can only hope that means it's time to eat. I catch up to Rosario, thinking about attempting to speak, but decided better of it by the persistent scowl painted on her face.

We make it into the chow hall and I fall in line. My beige colored tray is filled with white oatmeal that smells like sulfur, and I am given a single plastic cup of water that doesn't look filtered at all. When I turn to find a spot to sit, I notice that my silent roommate is by herself.

I make my way over to her table and sit down. Taking a bite before I decide better of it and figure out it doesn't taste as bad as it smells. "Eat slowly."

My ears are burning as I hear Rosario speak for the first time. "What?"

"Your stomach will swell if you eat or drink too fast."

"I know that, but why are you telling me?"

"Forget I said anything." She scarves down her food and makes a move to get up. *Great job, Gwen. You scared her off when she was trying to help.*

"Wait, sorry." She sits back down and looks at me with the same glower as before. "I just wasn't expecting, well, I'm not sure."

"You were expecting me to be cruel because you are human and I am not?" I nod. "Well, seeing as you will be dead at the end of the week, I see no point."

"Why does everyone keep saying that?"

"Because it's true. No human survives the first round."

"Well, I know how to fight."

"So did the others, but I am sure you saw their remnants before walking inside here." I grimace at the memory. "By the look on your face, I suspect that is a yes. Anyway, I am Rosario. Or as the guards say, eight-one-two-A."

"Nice to meet you. My name is Gwen. Or just like you, eight-one-two." She raises a brow. "What? Is the number already taken?"

"No, it's just I didn't expect you to introduce yourself as a commoner."

"And why's that?"

"Because you're a princess, are you not?"

I let out a breath. "Not anymore. I'm just another number."

"Good to know." After we continued our meal, I'm grateful for that conversation.

The rest of the week went by too quickly and I soon got used to the routine of the place. Wake up, inspection, meal, back to our cell and put on repeat for lunch and dinner.

It's I night before the fight I'm a bundle of nerves laying on my bed staring at the ceiling. "Stop fidgeting. You'll need to sleep for tomorrow."

"I'll sleep when I am dead."

"I like you are already in that mindset." We go back to being silent and I feel like I should ask her some questions that only a shifter could answer.

"Hey, Rosario, have you ever seen a mating ritual or a mating bond before?"

"Once." She answers quickly.

"What happens?"

"Why so curious?" I know she hasn't heard about everything if she wants to know why I am asking.

"You knew I was a princess when I came here, but I guess you don't know why besides the fact that your king wants all humans dead and enslaved." I wait to see if she will interrupt. "The shifter prince told me I was his mate, which was unbelievable at first, but I felt drawn to him and thought, why not? When I allowed myself to believe it, we consummated it and I thought I felt something connected to him within me. I thought it was a lie, but how could it be?"

"Honestly, I don't know, but that doesn't sound like a mating bond or ritual." I hear the bed creak and then my own dips as she moves to sit with me. "What I am about to tell is something I haven't spoken about in five years."

"Okay." I can see the hesitation on her face, but I wait, giving her time to muster up the courage to talk about what is clearly painful.

"Five years ago, I found my mate. She was my best friend, and I was beyond happy that my dragon claimed her only when it came time for the ritual. I was a nervous wreck. Selena's dragon claimed me too, and the ritual started, and our bond snapped into place. That's where this came from."

I look down at the intricate designs covering her right arm. "You get a tattoo marking your bond?"

She nods before continuing. "Each couple is different. We were so happy."

"What happened?"

"She was killed by her ex the next morning."

"I'm so sorry."

She laughs a half-hearted one. "That's why I am here. I killed him, but I couldn't save her because he used a shifter blade."

Something about that sentence made me think about the times I kissed, he who shall not be named, and the way he healed. "Can mates heal one another?"

"Amongst other things. We can share power, too."

"What does that mean?"

"Every shifter can summon fire, but there are other abilities we have too. There are too many to explain, but for example, along with my power, I can get inside people's minds and send them to an alternate reality where they feel everything as if it were real. Only inside their brains while their body remains in whatever surroundings they were in."

"Is that how you killed?" She nods in answer, and I am even more confused than before.

"Can shifters siphon magic from others without being mates?"

"Why do you want to know that?"

I blew out a breath, my loose strands moving out of my eyes. "Because nothing happened between me and the prince like you described except, he was wounded and then he kissed me and was healed."

"That's not possible. You're a human, aren't you?"

I wasn't sure if I should tell her about the power because I haven't had access to it since my capture, but I didn't see the harm. It wasn't like I was fighting her tomorrow. "I don't know what or who I am anymore. One second I am a normal human ready to take my place as queen and the next I am being whisked into the world of shifters and killers and shooting lightning out my hands."

"What? Did you say lightning?"

"Yes. Al- the prince said it wasn't anything he has ever heard a shifter be able to do before, so I don't think I am one. But then you said shifters can heal and power share with each other, so now I don't know."

She was quiet for a few minutes before finally speaking. "Well shit, I guess that explains why I didn't have the desire to kill you. You aren't fully human by the sound of it."

"You would've killed me? Just like that?" She shrugs before breaking out into a laugh, and I hit her arm with my pathetic excuse for a pillow.

"Whatever you are, I just hope you don't die tomorrow."

"Why?"

"Because I actually like you." I know I shouldn't let my guard down, but there is something about Rosario that brings me comfort.

"Thanks." she jumps down before bidding me goodnight and I let my eyes flutter close although it seems pointless as the irrational images coursing through my brain won't let me sleep.

CHAPTER 16

ALEX

IT'S BEEN TWO WEEKS since I watched Gwen get dragged out of here with my lies being the last words she heard leave my lips.

And now, she might die. Locknite gives you five days for change, which is surprising, but that is because it wasn't ruled by my father. Locknite was its own kingdom with one master; The Warden.

Father sent prisoners there because he knew that fate was worse than death. You fight to survive and that's it. I know Gwen can fight, but she will go up to the worst of the worst criminals. Shifters like me that are ruthless and give no shits if you are female or otherwise.

That's why I find myself in my brother's presence again. "Are you ready to keep your word?"

He sips on his whiskey, while sitting taut in his chair that overlooks the arena below. To add to my punishment, Father made me attend today's fight and said I needed to watch the whore die. It took all my self-control not to punch him.

He nods. "She'll survive."

"Who is her opponent?"

"Morris Baine."

"The Terminator? Shit, how the hell is she going to survive him?" I scrub a hand through my hair, not caring that my emotions are showing.

"Don't you trust me, brother?"

"No, but you're all I got at the moment." I spoke the same words that Gwen did so long ago. "I can't lose her, Arthur."

He gets to his feet, finishing his drink before setting it down and walking to the exit. "Where are you going?"

He glances over his shoulder before answering, "To ensure your mate survives."

I swallow hard, unsure if I like the mischievous look in his eyes. Closing my eyes, I try to call on my dragon, but he remains quiet and I'm not sure if I will ever be able to call upon him again.

"Today should be interesting," Morgan's voice cut through the air as she moves to stand next to me. "Ready to witness the death of your former lover?"

She is baiting me, like usual, trying to see if I will falter in my pretenses, but I will not let my guard down around her ever again. She has proven where her true loyalties lie. "Yes."

A smirk forms on her face as we look down at the sand covered area. I have watched fights before, when I was younger, and father made us come. I didn't pay them any attention, really. My mind was already on the businesses of my growing kingdom in Sagittarian Court cities.

The businesses that haven't been on my mind since escaping

with Gwen to Valerian Court on our fruitless mission to find the relics and speak with the gods. Which brings me to my next question. "Morgan, what happened to the other two princesses that were in the village when you captured Gwen?"

"Wouldn't you like to know?" She smirks before sipping on some wine.

"Of course, that is why I asked."

"You'll see."

The knowing look she gives me unsettles me, and a dreadful thought crosses my mind. "They're here too, aren't they?"

"The Valerian yes, she was intercepted when she was returning to give Gwen the Frozen Star relic. The Arian princess slipped through our fingers, but do not fret. We'll have her and her Autumn Star soon enough."

"Father is collecting all the relics?"

"Yes."

"For his armies?"

"Why are you so interested suddenly?"

I need to be careful how I answer her question. I come up with what any loyal son would say, despite how untrue it is. "Because if I am to join the fight, I want to know who will be on our side and how much power we will have."

"Then yes, he is. But he can explain his reasons. I'm not a messenger, just a general."

The doors open at her last words and in comes my father with his small entourage of guards and The Warden. "The show will start soon, Sire."

"Good, the sooner that human whore is dead, the sooner I can deliver her head to the Sagittarian Court and get this war started."

I don't have time to respond to that as the booming of The

Warden's voice reverberates off the walls and the lights go out everywhere except the arena below. "This will be a fight to the death. Our opponents will not stop until one is dead. Let the games begin."

My heart stops as I see her tiny figure walk out with no weapon in her hand and I do everything in my power to stop myself from running to her. The feeling of a hand on my shoulder makes me break my gaze and I look at my twin, who gives me a nod and I let a shuddering breath go.

"She'll survive." He whispers low enough for only me to hear. "I guarantee it."

GWEN

My stomach is in twisted knots as I stand on the outside of the doors that will lead into the arena.

Two guards stand posted just on the outside of the arched tunnel, obviously not worried about any attempt I might make at escaping, because where the hell will I go?

"Nervous?" The familiar smooth voice makes me still. "You don't have to look at me, although if you intend to insult me, remember what I said before about that?"

"Come to wish me luck?" I ask with no ounce of bite that I intended.

His body is so close to mine, his moonflower and ash scent is overwhelming, but instead of making me nervous, it has a calming effect. "I came to offer you my help."

His whispered words kiss my neck, eliciting a shiver. "A little too late for that."

"No, it's not." I laugh at the ridiculous notion. "Don't move."

I feel his hands brush my hips as he presses his chest to my back. "What are you doing?"

"Easy, just relax and listen to me."

"Not unless you get your hands off me." I snap at him.

"Keep that aggression, Sunshine. You're going to need it. Now, listen to me-"

"Why should I?"

"Because I will help you survive this." I quiet, my brain fighting with the urge to ignore him and listen to him. "By your silence, I guess you're ready to listen to me."

"Do you have to touch me?"

"Yes."

"Why?"

"Because, to the guards, it looks like I am having my way with you. They know not to disturb me. As long as you stay quiet and listen, this will be over, and I won't have to smell your vile scent any longer."

I go to speak, but he silences me with a tightening grip on my hips. "Speak."

"I know you have magic inside of you, but you don't know how to control it, so listen to me and you just might. When the instinct to flee kicks in, ignore it. Face your attacker head on, do not back down and your power will come forth to protect you."

"How can you possibly know that?"

His arms move to my shoulders and skate down my arms, my skin rises with the sensation. And I almost lean into him. "Because you are the unexpected."

He is gone before I have time to ask more questions and the bars open as I make my way into the arena. The lights are bright, blinding the seating area as I look up and then an announcer starts the beginning of the fight.

My opponent stands tall, with an eye patch covering his right one and thick muscles riddled with scars and tattoos. His horns are red, one shorter than the other, and his wings are flexed. The bastard is big as fuck and I desperately want to shrink back, but I stand my ground.

"Are you going to stand there or fight?" He growls and I cross my arms over my chest, planting my feet. Which could be a mistake. He smirks and then charges towards me with a fist. *Stand your ground and your power will come.*

Expert advice if it would've worked. My body is knocked ten feet back when his fists connect with my jaw. I spit blood on the sand and struggle to get to my feet. When the shifter comes barreling at me again, I decide fuck it, and take flight.

Stumbling forward, I get my balance and sprint, looking around for any sign of a weapon I could use to help me, but there is nothing. I skid to a halt at the sight of him landing. "I have wings, girl. You cannot outrun me. Surrender, and I will make it quick."

"Never." I spit out and ready my fist. *If I cannot escape, I will fight.*

"Brave and stupid, considering I have at least two hundred pounds of muscle on you."

"Are you going to talk or fight?" I snarl and he smirks, charging forward again. This time, I dodge his swing, rolling forward and thrusting my fist straight into his crotch.

"Fuck." he curses and I get to my feet just in time to jump on his back and loop my arms around his neck. "Get off me."

I lock my arm tight, dodging each swipe of his hand as his wings flap with his struggle. When I think I have won, he pauses and then falls backward, crushing me into the dirt with his body weight.

The breath is knocked out of me, and my body goes slack. He is quick to turn over and his fist meets my face again. One after the other as my bones crack, telling me something is broken. My blood has a copper tang to it as my eyes blur and the world goes silent around me.

This is what death is like. My body is going numb, although I can still see the fists pounding into me from above. I want to let go, to let myself meet the gods and be reunited with my parents, but something inside of me sparks.

Face your attacker head on, do not back down and your power will come forth to protect you. His voice echoes in my mind and I reach down inside of me, gripping onto the spark before my hands move on its own.

The shifter's eyes widen as I halted his assault with pink sparks dancing around my fingers that are gripped tightly around his wrists. "How?"

I push him off me, down to his knees, while I stare into his eyes. Seeing my reflection in them. Lightning dances on the edges of my skin and the power surges into a ball in front of me, waiting for my command. "Because I'm Princess Gwen of the Sagittarian Court and I will not back down."

The ball of power surges forward, connecting with the shifter's chest and going straight through him until stopping just on the other side. I release my grip on him and he falls forward with a thud. Looking around, the lights dim and the crowded arena is revealed to me.

When my eyes land on the two blue ones four levels higher than me, I don't hesitate in my next attack, sending my ball of power crashing into the traitor prince and his father. "Kill her!"

My power is at the edge of my skin, and I won't let it falter again, not now, never. Forming another ball in my hands, I aim it towards the entrance, and it explodes in a cloud of rubble and smoke. Sprinting forward, I prepare myself to be greeted by the guards, only to see them lying on the ground with wounds.

Moving through the debris, I go the opposite direction I was taken, praying it will lead me to an exit only to stop short when I reach a dead end. "Fuck."

"So close." I seize up at the sound of her voice. "Did you honestly think you could break out of here?"

I turn to face her. Not wanting to answer or give her a chance to attack and let my power charge at her, but she dodges it by throwing her own power over me. "What happened, Morgan? You were my friend once."

She growls, flames dancing along her fingers. "That was before you killed Mordrid."

"I had no control over my power and you knew that. If you want to hear an apology, you will not get one because there is no need for one when she tried to kill me."

"And now you're going to kill me?" She questions.

"I don't want to, but to defend myself, yes."

"Fine. But let's do this like actual women. No magic." I don't know what she is up to, but clearly my power scares her if she wants it off the table, but I agree.

"I will agree to an honorable fight."

She removes her leather jacket before getting into a fighting stance. We circle each other before she moves first. I block her attack and push her out of the way. "Don't pull your punches, Gwen."

If that is what she wants, then so be it. We engage again. This time I let her land the blow to my already swollen face while I land one right on her temple. A dangerous spot, but one I know will knock her unconscious. I catch her as she falls, setting her down gently. "I'm surprised."

I look up, my fists ready to fight the next person, but when I see who it is, I lower a fraction. "I don't want to kill your sister. She is just trying to avenge the death of her lover. There is honor in that."

Arthur hums before leaning against the wall and putting his hands in his pocket. "What is the next part of your plan, Sunshine?"

"First, stop calling me that. There is nothing sunny about me. And second, since you're here, you're going to help me escape and then you're going to get a friend of mine out, too."

"Oh, and why would I do that?"

"Because why would you want me to win that fight if you didn't want to see me escape?"

He runs his tongue over his teeth before sucking them and shrugging. "Just wanted to see your power for myself."

"Fine. Are you going to help me or not?"

"Not." he turns around and walks away from me, but then stops to look over his shoulder. "Good luck, Sunshine."

I watch as he disappears into the shadows, and I snap out of my stupor to look for the next way out. Running forward, I look out in the corridor, but it's crammed with guards. All searching for me. "We have orders to kill."

Well shit, can't get out. I think about using my power to break through the wall, but I can't be sure what's on the other side, so I squeeze myself into an alcove hidden by shadows and wait.

An hour passes and I don't hear the shuffling of feet or speaking of guards and bravely step out of the alcove, only to be ensnared by powerful arms and a familiar scent. Ashe and fire.

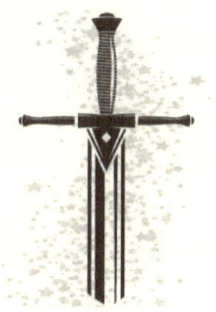

CHAPTER 17

GWEN

"Don't move, princess."
His lips brush my ear and my body reacts like it did the first time we met.

Only my brain fights it, and I sink my teeth into his hand. He releases his hold and I elbow him in the gut before rearing my fist back to punch him. Only the blow doesn't land and he has me pinned to the wall with his knee between my legs and my arms locked in his grip.

"Fucking hell, Gwen. I will not hurt you."

"Could've fooled me." I snarl.

"I know what I said before, but I can explain just as soon as we get out of here." He is playing me again, I know he is.

"Just leave me alone."

"Gwen, please I…"

"You what? Love me? No, you don't. Nothing we had was real. Let me go, Alexxander."

He swallows hard before shaking his head. "I'm getting you out of here and then we are going to talk."

I search for the lie but find nothing but truth in his eyes. "Once we leave these walls, I never want to see you again."

He ignores my words and then motions for me to follow. We crouch low, and I follow him down winding corridors until we finally stumble on another dead end. "Great, now what?"

"Patience, princess." He shifts his hand forward, pressing into the wall, and I watch with amazement as it dissipates, and the outside world is revealed to me.

I jump forward, only to be jerked back by a grip on my neck. "Fuck."

"I will not hurt you, Gwen, but I can't let you just walk away without hearing me out."

Against my better judgment, I agree, because his touch still affects me, his scent still engulfs me, and no matter what, I cannot deny my attraction to him. "Fine."

He releases his grip on my neck, only to wrap me up in his arms and then we take off to the sky. The rushing of the winds sends cool waves of air over me, and I close my eyes. Soaking in the freedom of the outside world. My thoughts drift to Rosario and my friends. Guilt hits me and I know I need to help them somehow.

"Open your eyes, princess." I do as he says and find my feet planted on hard ground and then notice we are on the top of a mountain range.

"Why up here?"

He smirks, and I hate the way my stomach flutters at the familiarity of it. "It was the only way to ensure you didn't run off before I had the chance to say my peace."

I cross my arms under my breast and look down at my feet.

"So, speak."

"Everything I said to you in that throne room was a lie. I never once faked anything with you, and I said all that to keep my father from killing you right on the spot."

"And the part about us being mates?"

"I swear to you that was true. My dragon claimed you, Gwen. Everything I feel for you is real."

I remembered what Rosario said about the ritual, and the tattoos, but the look on his face tells me he truly believes it, even if I don't. "We aren't mates, Alexxander. We never were and never will be."

"How can you say that?"

I tuck a loose strand behind my ear before answering. "Because I can never trust you with my heart again. You broke me in worse ways than anyone else ever could and I..." My voice stutters and he takes a step towards me, cupping my cheek.

"Please don't say this is the end."

"There are more important things I need to focus on than us. My power control, my people, my friends. There is no room for you anymore."

I can see what my words are doing to him, because *his* words did the same thing to me, only this time there are no lies spoken. "Baby, please. Give me a chance to prove myself."

He leans forward, a breath of space between our lips. "I can't forgive you, Alexxander."

I press my lips to his, allowing us both this last kiss, this goodbye. "Don't push me away, baby."

He deepens it, his tongue touching the seam of my lips, and I grant him permission. I moan at the feel of him, the taste of him on my tongue, but I break away, not wanting to let it go any further than that. "Goodbye, Alex."

"I won't stop fighting for you, for us. Whatever it takes, Gwen. I'll kill my father and anyone else who stands in your way." Even though I know I shouldn't, I stop in my steps and look over my shoulder. "I'm not saying you have to take me back, but please give me the chance to earn your trust again."

"Goodbye, Alex."

I don't look back as I leave my former lover behind, as well as solidifying the wall around my heart.

I make it half-way down the mountain before needing to stop and take a break.

My lightning dances around my fingers and I love the feeling of it. "Hello, Sunshine."

I jump to my feet, my power ready to attack, until I see him come out of the shadows with his hands raised. "Easy, I'm not here to hurt you."

"Then why are you here?"

"Is that any way to thank me?" He feigns hurt, but I roll my eyes.

"Some help you were. I nearly died."

"Ah, but you didn't. You listened to me and your power came through." He eyes me up and down and I think I see respect on his face before it goes into a smirk. "And what power do you have?"

It comes out as a purr.

"Yeah, whatever. You can leave now."

"Easy. I am on your side. I want to help you rid this world of my father."

"Why?" I don't believe him. I can't let my guard down around these shifters. Not anymore.

"My reasons are mine alone, but you need my help to get your revenge."

"No. I want nothing to do with shifters anymore."

"Even if it means saving your friend." That caught my attention. "I see the look in your eyes. You wish me to elaborate, so I will. Your dear Valerian Princess is locked up back in Locknite."

"What? How is she alright? Gods, we have to save her." He smirks and I realize I used the word we.

"We will. You need to train first. You are powerful, but you have no control. Agree to let me train you and I will help you in your conquest to defeat all the evil of the world."

I eyed him suspiciously but thought about my choices. "One step out of line and I will fry you where you stand. Control or not."

"Fair enough. Shall we shake on it?"

I push to my feet and close the small amount of distance between us, holding out my right hand. "We do."

He smirks before I see one of his talons elongate and he slices his palm, "This is how we make deals, Sunshine. Take it or leave it."

"Just do it." I maintain eye contact with him as he cuts my flesh and then I feel the warmth of our blood mixing as small embers alight behind his eyes before they are washed away again.

It's been a week since I escaped Locknite.

Arthur informed me that Tori got captured the day after I did while bringing the Frost Star with her.

"We are going to need his help." Arthur states while we look at the blueprints on Locknite.

"Arthur, don't be a dick." I groan while ignoring the twinge my heart makes at the thought of his twin. "I think we should be able to break in the way I got out."

I turn to look at Arthur, and he shakes his head in disagreement. "No way. After you and my brother escaped, they sealed off everything. The only way in is through force."

I let out a sigh, "Don't worry, Sunshine, after I am done with you, no one will stop you."

"It's been a week and I am no closer to calling on it than I was fighting your sister."

He smirks at me. I catch sight of a dimple on his right cheek pop. "You're cute when you get flustered."

I roll my eyes because, frankly, Arthur seems like one of those playboy types. "Stop attempting to flirt with me and help me figure out how we are going to get in and get out."

My gaze stays locked onto the inside perimeter of the building. Ten levels for inmates, but then there are all these other rooms that I have no clue what they are. I turn to ask Arthur, but stop as I feel his breath kissing my cheek.

"I wasn't flirting with you, Sunshine."

"Sure sounded like it." It comes out as a whisper.

He smirks again, his hand going to my cheek to turn me to look into his eyes. They are remarkably different from Alexxander's. A beautiful jade color. His face turns serious before he murmurs, "You'll know when I am flirting with you, *Gwenyfer.*"

We gaze at each other for a moment before I get to my feet. Not wanting to allow myself to get into a fight with my acquaintance. "I would like to shower now."

I turn away from him and move towards the bathroom. He doesn't say another word, which I am grateful for. Much like his brother, Arthur has a way with words that have me questioning my sanity.

The water is warm against my skin. I sink to the tub, bring my knees to my chest as I let the tears fall. Baby, please... Alex's pleading and broken voice runs on repeat in my head. I almost turned around and ran back into his arms.

You're my mate, princess and I choose you. How could he have said that to me? Made me feel wanted and loved. Only to rip my heart from my chest and stomp on it.

I bite my lip as the sob comes to life. My tears mixed with the spray, just as it has since we got to the Inn two days ago. The only time I let the betrayal of Alexxander show is when I am in here. Arthur would ask too many questions or talk shit, and I cannot handle that at the moment.

After ten more minutes, I finally stand, wash, and get out of the shower. With the water off, the steam fills the bathroom as I wrap a towel around my body. Drying off, I combed through my hair before applying lotion to my skin and adorning a sleep shirt and shorts.

Out in the bedroom, I see Arthur laying on the couch appearing to be asleep. Not disturbing him, I pull back the covers and slip under the cotton sheets, ready to sleep. Only, it won't come. It never does.

"Something on your mind, Sunshine?"

"Sleep." I reply immediately.

"Then why are you tossing and turning so much?" He sounds aggravated and I know it's because of the noise I am making. "Do you need me to come over there and help you relax?"

"How could you possibly do that?" I don't get a response right away, but in the next second, I feel the bed dip. "What are you doing?"

"Easy, Sunshine. Lay back and just go with it."

I glare at him, my nostrils flaring. "Get out of my bed before I kick you out."

"Will you just shut up and roll over?"

"No." I answer, sitting up and crossing my arms.

"I will do nothing, Gwen. Ease up."

"Then why are you in this bed?"

He runs his hand through his shortened golden locks before answering. "When I was little, I used to have night terrors. My mom would lie in bed with me, saying she would protect me from the demons trying to attack my mind. I would be safe with her and that I could fall asleep."

Gods, this is really personal for him. "Why are you telling me this?"

"Because I have watched you night after night, tossing and turning because of your own demons, and I need sleep." A beat of silence passes before I lay back down and turn over.

There is movement behind me, and I realize he has to lie

down, too. "I can hear you thinking."

"This is so weird." I breathe out.

"Go to sleep, Sunshine."

Two Weeks after Locknite

"Focus, sunshine."

"I'm trying." I hate how whiny I sound, but I am frustrated beyond belief and my period cramps are killing me. "We've been practicing this move for two weeks. If I don't have it down by now, then why should we keep going at it?"

The move I am talking about is connecting with the most triggering emotion I have, gripping on to it, and summoning the power in my hands.

Arthur stands with his hands in his front pockets, his face holding that usual smirk. I swear his face remains frozen like that. He saunters closer to me, stepping behind me, before speaking. "Breathe, you should know by now I will not hurt you."

I nod and then I feel him press into my back, his hands on my shoulders while he whispers in my ear. "Close your eyes." I comply. "Breathe in and then out before focusing on a memory. It can be any memory."

I do as he says, my head running through various memories until I land on one.

My body is warm, and I feel more rested than I have in weeks. I feel something hard pressed against my back. A thick arm is wrapped around my waist while soft breath kisses my neck. The scent of ash and moonflower washed over me. I open my eyes, a silent panic happening at the reality of this situation.

Arthur must have cuddled me in my sleep, and I feel his erection pressing into my ass. Should I move? Do I want to? Fuck.

"Open your eyes, Sunshine." Arthur's voice cuts through my memory, bringing me back to the present as I open my eyes. "Look at your hands."

My gaze shifts as I lift my hands. Pink lightning dances around my fingers, electrifying my dark complexion. "I did it!"

I turn around, throwing my arms around Arthur's neck and pausing, realizing what I did. I take a step back. "Sorry, just got a little excited. Did I hurt you?"

He clears his throat before shaking his head from side to side. "So, what memory did you use?"

Fuck. I can't tell him I was thinking about the time I woke up in his arms. "Just a happy memory."

He eyes me suspiciously before running a hand through his hair. "Now, practice that for the next hour."

"Wait, where are you going?"

"Recon." He answers and before I can protest, he is gone. Arthur doesn't use his wings. I have never seen them, and I am curious if they match his brother's golden ones.

I do as he ordered, and I feel confident enough by the end. Sifting through various happy memories, and most definitely avoiding the one about us. By the time I am done, I am so exhausted; I knock out for a nap on the bed.

Why am I back in that throne room? Alexxander stands in front of me, his blue eyes full of hate and disgust as he cuts my heart into pieces. "... you were so desperate to be loved, to be

*chosen, that you made easy prey. All I had to do was dangle
the idea that I was your mate and you jumped up, begging me
to fuck you like the whore you are."*

His words were venom cutting straight through me like a
thousand knives all at once. "You're lying."

"Gwen! Wake up, Sunshine!"

I snap awake, sweat coating my features as the smell of
burning fabric hits my nose. Looking down, I see the bed is
burnt to a crisp around me.

"What the fuck were you dreaming about?"

I lock eyes on Arthur's, his jade ones full of concern, and
my answer gets locked inside my throat. Jumping to my feet,
I race to the bathroom, hurling up my lunch. Warm hands run
down my back, pulling my hair out of the way as I empty my
stomach. "Easy, Sunshine."

"Go away, Arthur." It comes out in a croak.

"Who's going to hold your hair for you if I leave?" There is
humor in his tone, and I know he is trying to cheer me up, but
I don't know why.

I wipe my mouth on my sleeve before turning to look at
him. "Why are you here, Arthur?"

"Because I need to be."

"Bullshit. Give me the truth or just leave."

"You're so feisty. I can see why my brother fell for you." I
cringe at that, and he notices, but doesn't comment. Instead, he
reaches out, caresses my cheek slightly. "You're unexpected,
Gwenyfer. There is no one in existence that has your power
and as much as I hate to admit this. I need your help to take
down my father."

"Why?"

"I am broken. I have minor magic. What I have, I use it

to glamor myself. I am not strong enough to defeat him by myself."

I wasn't sure what to say to that. He was showing me another vulnerability of his. Beneath all that smirking and charming tongue is a damaged soul, just like mine. "Why me? Why do I have this power, yet I am still human?"

"I don't know, but I will help you find out if that is what you want to do." I saw the sincerity in his eyes and heard it in his voice.

"No. The most important thing is getting control, finding a way into Locknite, saving Tori and Rosario, then destroying your father."

He smirks again before cupping my chin. "There's my brave warrior. Get cleaned up so we can plot and eat."

Three Weeks Since Locknite

I am getting stronger with my control and my body feels it too. So far, I have control over happiness, using that emotion to call onto my magic with just a happy thought instead of going through the entire breathing technique beforehand. I mostly think of times with Tori and Diliha.

At the thought of them, I worry because there has been no word from anyone about Diliha. At least Arthur has someone monitoring Tori while she is in Locknite. "Arthur, have you heard anything about Diliha?"

He looks concerned, as if he knows something, but doesn't want to voice it. "Arthur?"

"I will tell you, but only if you promise to remain in control."

"What?" Panic erupts inside of me, because the only reason he would want me in control is because it's something bad. "Spit it out, Arthur."

"Fuck." He runs his hand through his hair. I notice he does this when he is nervous. "There is a rumor she is dead."

My world stops. Everything is silent as the word dead repeats in my mind. "She can't be."

He swallows hard before doing that stupid hair thing again. "I know. That's why I looked into it. There is another rumor that she is in Locknite or in hiding."

"Has your person seen her?"

"No. No one fit her description. As far as I know, Princess Victoria is the only human there."

I rub my head, breathing through the panic. *Okay, so she's alive. I know it. I won't believe she is dead until I see a body.*

"Okay. Have you figured out how to get into Locknite?"

"Yes, but-"

"But? No, there can't be a *but*, Arthur."

"Just shut up and listen, will you?" I bite my lip and nod. "We need Alexxander's help."

"No!" I exclaim. "If you can't do this without him, then I will just do it by myself."

"Don't be an idiot, Gwenyfer." I turn and march towards the bedroom door. A firm grip on my bicep has me stopping and turning towards Arthur. "I promise I won't let him hurt you again."

"You can't promise the impossible, Arthur."

He leans forward, his jade eyes boring into mine. "I will kill him if he hurts you."

My breath catches with the intensity of his glare, confusing emotions surface and I shake my head. "Let me go, Arthur. I need some space. Time to think. I'll be back tonight."

Reluctantly, he lets go. "Keep your hood up and don't talk to anyone."

I don't respond, just walk away from him and out into the vacant corridor, not stopping until I am sitting on top of the roof.

Looking up to the sky, the sun is setting, and I know the stars will come soon. A rogue tear falls as I think about my parents, wishing they were here to guide me on the right path. *Mom, Dad, I don't know if you can hear me, but I am so confused right now. I have magic, our people are in danger, and my best friends are on the path to death.*

"And it's all my fault." I mutter the last part out loud.

A bitter taste develops in my mouth as I think about everything that has happened the last couple of months. Starting with the attacks within the city, the Lord Regent, Prince Mauris, Alexxander, and everything after. It's all been focused on me, and my friends got put in danger because of it.

Swallowing down the self-pity, I make the decision that this fight would be for them. For my people. To give everyone the right to live in peace without fear of tyranny and death.

Pushing to my feet, I make my way back to the room where I find Arthur sitting on the couch, drink in hand. "If he hurts me, I will kill you after you kill him."

He smirks at me before closing the distance in two strides. "Now there is my feisty warrior."

CHAPTER 18

ALEX

I SIT ON A stool in some tavern in the middle of nowhere and drown myself in whiskey.

"Hello, brother." I don't have to look to my left to know who it is. "One month and you are still as pathetic as you were when I found you on that mountaintop."

"Go away." It slurs out and I know I am the drunkest I have been in a while.

"Come now, baby brother. I figured you'd be delighted to see me, seeing as I am the one who saved your dear one."

"Haven't you heard? We broke up."

He chuckles, but I ignore him. "You've always been a sore loser. But I didn't expect you to give up so easily. I know if I had someone like her, I would never let her go."

"What are you doing here besides pissing me off?" I growl and look at him.

"I'm here to help you. I hear your ex-lover is searching for the relics. Two of which are locked up tight in father's castle and the other two remain in the other courts."

I shrug, uncaring. "So?"

"I figured you'd want an update on her."

That catches my attention, and I turn my entire body to look at him. "Have you been watching her?"

"Just keeping my end of our deal. Oh, and by the way, you still owe me something."

I laugh, a deep belly laugh because I figured that was why he was here. "Alright, what do you want? You want out the deal? Fine by me. She is safe and unharmed."

He raises a brow before speaking. "Yes. Recant the deal and our business is concluded."

"Really?"

"Yes." I eye him suspiciously, but I don't see the typical mischief in his eyes like I usually do. I hold out my hand and he grips it, then I recite the words of recantation and our deal is done.

"What now?" I ask before gulping down the rest of the whiskey.

"Now, you sober up and help me defeat our father while winning your lost love back."

"Excuse me?" He pats me on the back before tossing some coin on the bar.

"Let's get moving. We don't have a lot of time before Gwen is on the move again. Sneaky little thing she is." I get up from my seat and follow my brother out of the tavern.

We go about two buildings over before he grabs me and guides me into another one; I don't fight him, partially because I am trashed and the other because why the hell should I? He practically carries me up two flights of stairs until we come across a room.

Once inside, I halt at the sight before me. "Hello, Alexxander."

"Gwen? What the hell are you doing here?"

"Wow, what a greeting."

"He's drunk." Arthur states before walking over to her and whispering something in her ear. My blood boils at the sight of their closeness. I sober up almost immediately.

"Somebody tell me what the hell is going on."

Gwen steps up to me. She looks just as beautiful as the last time I saw her, only healed. "Arthur, please give us a moment."

My brother leaves the room, and I don't understand how or why they seem so friendly suddenly. The door closes and I move towards her, not stopping until I have my arms wrapped around her. "I've missed you so much."

She steps away from me and looks me in the eye before breaking me all over again. "Nothing has changed, Alexxander. We are not together, but I called you here because I need your help."

I hate the sound of her using my full name, but that she needs me gives me hope. "I would do anything for you."

"I know, that's why I need you to help me gain control of my magic. I asked Arthur first but-"

"Wait. You went to him before me?" My tone doesn't hide the anger and jealousy that I feel. "What is going on between the two of you?"

"Nothing. He's just been there for me when you haven't."

"Because you said goodbye!" I yell, but just as I knew she would, she stands her ground.

"And I meant it. Gods, Alex, if I knew you were going to act like a jealous ex, I would've never asked you to come."

She's right, because that is how I feel at the moment. "Look, if this will not work with you and your brother, I don't want you around. Either help or get out of my life for good."

Fucking hell, this woman knows how to cut me deep, but if she thinks I am going to let my twin wheedle his way into her heart without a fight, then so be it. "Fine."

"One screw up, one toe out of line, and you're done." She states and my cock jumps at the sound of her voice.

"Agreed."

The door opens and my brother walks in with a smirk on his smug face. "Well, is my baby brother going to join the fight?"

"He is." I answer for myself. Then I know I need a conversation with Arthur, too. "Gwen, please allow me a moment with my brother."

She looks at him, the same way she did me once when she was concerned about my well-being, and it breaks me. "It's okay, Sunshine. He won't hurt me."

Sunshine? What the fuck? "I need to fetch some supplies, anyway."

Once she is gone, I wait until the last of her steps fade before I let my fist fly. "What the fuck are you doing?"

Arthur spits blood on the floor before answering me. "Helping to defeat our father. What does it look like?"

"It looks like you're moving in on my woman. My mate."

"Last I checked," we are now nose to nose, chest to chest, "she wasn't yours. Never was."

"Is this how it's going to be?" I snarl at him, my wings flexing behind me.

"It wasn't, but now that I see how pissed you are, I might just wheedle my way into her heart. Just to piss you off and when she chooses me over you, just know that it was your fault."

The door opens, and he backs away, but not before Gwen catches the tension between us. "Okay, judging by the testosterone wafting into the air, I am going to guess you two did more than talk. But whatever, I don't care. Just as long as it doesn't mess with my mission."

The door closes and I look at her again, the aching in my chest growing and the need to embrace her again pulsing through me. "Come, sit down so we can discuss this plan."

We take our seats, both of us on either side of her as she lays out the world map. "First things first. We free the prisoners from Locknite, including Tori. Then we need to find Diliha and the other relics. Meanwhile, you both will train me in certain things."

"Whatever you say, Sunshine."

"Anything for you, Princess." She looks between the both of us before shrugging.

"Okay, that's it for tonight. Go to bed, sober up, and we will begin training tomorrow. As far as we know, Tori is safe for now."

"How do you know?" I ask her.

"I have a man on the inside looking out for her. She is good for another three months before it's her turn to fight." Arthur answers, and I don't like the sound of that. I hate him being here, but for Gwen, I push that aside.

"Good to know." The room goes quiet. Arthur and I continue to stare at each other until Gwen clears her throat.

"Okay, I'm going to shower and go to bed. Seeing as we only have one room-"

"I have one." I interrupt.

"Good, go sleep in it. I'll watch over her." Arthur states.

"Fat chance, brother." I retorts.

"Gods, get out of here, Alexxander. Arthur and I have been sharing the room for a month."

"What?" I snap at her. She rubs her temples and Arthur gives me a smug smirk.

"I'm not dealing with these. Goodnight. If you kill each other, I will not be held responsible." She disappears into the bathroom, but I don't move.

"I hate you." I growl at him.

"Good. Now do as our princess asked. Run along, sober up. She needs us both." I push past him, knocking my shoulder into him, but I can't help the insult building inside of me.

"I'm leaving, but that's only because I know she would never fuck a man like you. A shifter with no magic, it's laughable." With the last of my words, I make my way to my room and quickly strip out of my clothes to take a long shower.

This is our chance. Don't let him fuck it up. You will be mine again, Gwen. No matter what it takes.

GWEN

The shower soothes my aching muscles and I lather myself with the floral scented soap. I rub my shoulder muscles until I feel someone else behind me.

Lips press against my neck as a hard male body presses into me. I moan at the feeling, "Fuck, princess, make that noise again and this won't last long."

I freeze, turning around to face him. "Alex, what are you doing here?"

"Taking what's mine." His lips crash against me in a claiming possessiveness, as if he is a man starved and I kiss him back. Missing the flavor of him, the feel of his skin pressing against mine. When I break it, my breathing is hard, only it isn't Alex anymore, it's Arthur.

I snap awake, sweat coating my skin and the evidence of my dream coating my sex and thighs. Fucking hell, a sex dream. I need to shut that shit down right now. I look over at the settee where Arthur has taken up residence since we moved into this room a month ago. Tossing the covers off my body, I slip out of bed and move to the bathroom.

Turning on the faucet, I splash cool water on my face and neck before taking another quick, cold shower and slipping my clothes on. When I step out of the bathroom, I try to remain quiet as I make my way to the door. "Nightmares again, Sunshine?"

I turn around. Arthur is right behind me, his moonflower scent overwhelming me and the dream flashes in my mind again. "Something like that."

He smirks, that half smirk that allows a dimple to show up. "You want to talk about it?"

I can't talk to you about my sex dream. "Not really. I just need some fresh air."

I need space. "I'll walk you out."

"No." I snap. Him being close to me is not something I need right now.

"It's not safe for you to be alone out there."

"Right. Okay, just keep your distance and I will pretend you aren't there."

"Whatever you say, Sunshine." And he does just that as I make my way up to the roof. I don't notice him at all while I look up to the stars and wonder if my parents are looking down on me.

After a while, I look over my shoulder and see Arthur not too far away doing the same thing as me. "Want to talk about it?"

He looks over at me before pushing to his feet and taking the spot next to me. "My mother is up there. As are your parents. Do you think they hear us?"

"I don't know, but I like to think they do." I answer. Then the next thing to fall out of my mouth is the word vomit. "Why do you and your brother hate each other so much?"

"That's a long story, Sunshine, and not one I like to voice, but I am sure you can persuade him to tell you."

"Well, I don't want to hear it from him." His jade eyes meet mine in a heated gaze before they cool back down.

"Every story has three sides to it. Mine, his, and the truth." He reaches out to caress my cheek. "Whether you hear from him or me, it won't matter. In his eyes, I am in the wrong, and in my eyes, he is."

"Well, let me base my conclusion on it." He gives me a soft smile before pulling back.

"We should head back inside. The sun will rise soon, and we have a long day ahead of us." I get to my feet, hating that I am no closer than I was a month ago to getting to know him better.

"Right." We make it back inside just in time to run into Alex in the hall who eyes us suspiciously, but I roll my eyes because he has no right to make assumptions like that.

"Did I miss the invite?" He asks with ice lacing his tongue.

"No. I had a bad dream and needed air. Arthur was just my back up. Anyway, we should get inside the room so we can discuss our journey north." I don't wait for him to speak. I push my way inside my room and, as they follow, I plop down on my chair. "We will need to be stealthy about it, which means no flying. I can train along the way, use my lightning while we walk through the Fields of Constellinia. We'll bypass your father's palace and head straight to Locknite."

"Okay, what about us getting noticed?" Alexxander asks.

"Disguise. You two can glamor yourself to look like anything, and Arthur said there is a way for you to push it onto someone else."

"Yes, but I have never done it." Alexxander confesses.

"I have." Arthur states, and the way his brother narrows his eyes has me confused.

"How, you have no magic?"

"What? Arthur, is that true?"

"It's partly true. I have magic. It's weak, but I'm still strong enough to charm us both. But I already told her that."

"Not for the journey we need to take." Alexxander states.

"Look, I don't care who does it. We just need it long enough to get out of the city. Once we are deep within the Fields, it won't matter. Got it?" I state and they both nod. "Good. Now that that is settled, there is one more issue."

"Okay?" They say in unison.

"From now on, I will sleep in my room by myself."

"What?"

"Did he do something?"

They both say, and I roll my eyes. "You two are idiots. No, I just need my space, and my privacy."

"Agreed." Alexxander states and I look at Arthur, who gives me a knowing smirk.

"Okay, but we have a condition, too." I was not expecting that. I nod for him to speak. "No other male or female may bed you."

"Excuse me? Who do you think you are telling me who I can and cannot take to my bed?" I snarl with a clenched fist.

"I'm going to have to agree with my brother on this one." I turn my glare towards my ex.

"And what am I supposed to do about my needs?" They look at each other, then look at me, both of their sets of unique eyes heating with lust. "You know what? I am more than capable of handling it on my own. Once this war is over, we cut ties with one another, and it won't matter who is in my bed."

After that embarrassingly long discussion, we finally pack up the provisions while Arthur and Alexxander come to an agreement on who will glamor me. My hair color goes from brown to blonde, my eyes hazel, and my skin is a lighter pigment.

We maneuver through the city without complication and make it to the edge of the Fields. "Are you sure you're ready for this?"

I am asking them both to betray their family and their people.

"Anything for you, Princess."

"I got your back, Sunshine."

We move forward, the journey will be long, and I have a lot to do before I master my power but with the help of these two, I know I will be ready when the time comes to save my world from the evil that threatens it.

TO BE CONTINUED...

AUTHOR NOTE

I really enjoyed writing this story. It was a wild ride and started out as a different story. This is my biggest book to date at 72,000 words. I hope the cliff-hanger wasn't too bad and you are excited about the next book.

If you are interested in discussing this book, please consider joining my reading group on Facebook.
Link: https://www.facebook.com/groups/1079372232891537/

C.M. Hano is a small-town author currently
residing in Louisiana. Her love for Adult Fantasy
inspires her to continue to create magical worlds
readers can escape to. She lives a charming life with
her husband and two daughters.

STAY IN TOUCH

Facebook: C. M. Hano
Twitter: @HanoCera
Instagram: @cerahano
TikTok: @cmhano_author
Reading Group: C. M. Hano's Reading Warriors

Also, By C. M. Hano

<u>World Of Dalaria</u>
YA-Fantasy

<u>The Princess Chronicles</u>
The Journey Begins
The Hollow Realm
The War Back Home

NA-Dark Fantasy
Blood Oath
Shadow Light

<u>LGBTQ NA-Fantasy</u>
TarotVerse
Xora
Whitfrost

<u>Sci-Fi NA-Fantasy</u>
<u>The Cursed Parlay</u>
The Cursed Parlay
Across The Starless Sky

<u>Reverse Harem Fantasy</u>
<u>World Of Zavinia</u>
Queen of Kings